This
Town
Sleeps

This Town Sleeps

A Novel

DENNIS E. STAPLES

COUNTERPOINT
Berkeley, California

Library of Congress Cataloging-in-Publication Data
Names: Staples, Dennis E., author.
Title: This town sleeps : a novel / Dennis E. Staples.
Description: Counterpoint Press : Berkeley, California, [2020]
Identifiers: LCCN 2019019472 | ISBN 9781640092846
Subjects: LCSH: Gay men—Fiction. | Ojibwa Indians—Minnesota—Fiction. |
    Murder—Investigation—Fiction. | Legends—Fiction. | Psychological
    fiction. | GSAFD: Mystery fiction.
Classification: LCC PS3619.T3675 T55 2020 | DDC 813/.6—dc23
LC record available at https://lccn.loc.gov/2019019472

Jacket design by Nicole Caputo
Book design by Jordan Koluch

COUNTERPOINT
2560 Ninth Street, Suite 318
Berkeley, CA 94710
www.counterpointpress.com

Printed in the United States of America
Distributed by Publishers Group West

10 9 8 7 6 5 4 3 2 1

This book is dedicated to my mother, Karen,
who taught me to read,
and to the memory of Jacob Grissom,
who taught me how to love.

I can

see how easy it is to confuse estrangement with
what comes before that, what's really just another
form of being lost, having meant to spell out—
wordlessly, handlessly—*I'm falling*, not *Sir,
I fell*

—CARL PHILLIPS, "The Greatest Colors
for the Emptiest Parts of the World"

This
Town
Sleeps

Indian Paintbrush

THE YOUNG MAN WAITED in the woods, and he thought of it like destiny.

Indian men were supposed to be warriors, watchers, killers, the young man thought. Survivors. His own life was a testament to that. Five hundred years since the end, and there were still tribes. Still warriors. Still a young man in the woods, holding a knife.

He had never used it for its intended purpose of skinning and carving deer, or any animal in the north woods that had the honor of dying for another's sustenance. The knife was clean, blade colored dark green and serrated like a birch leaf, and ready.

Another young man entered the forest. Just the two of us, he thought as he held the knife. Two survivors. Two living, breathing Ojibwe *ogichidaag* that the *chi-mookomaanag* had not killed yet.

Darkness hid the waiting warrior from the other, who did not see him approach or the knife as it entered his stomach, his chest, face, back. The young man felt as if he was painting, and each brushstroke ripped apart the tanned leather canvas in lines of sunset. This was art, and he was a flower. An Indian paintbrush. And his roots were being watered with blood.

One warrior walked out of the woods.

What Boys Do

I DON'T KNOW WHY I keep coming back here.

Geshig is a reservation town situated on a major highway about fifteen miles from Half Lake. The population sign reads 667, one digit from freaking out the superstitious and religious.

That's a common thing in Geshig. There are five churches, after all, including an Ojibwe-Christian fusion chapel that started as a Masonic brotherhood. The whites, the reds, the boxes for "other," and any remaining groups: all are superstitious here.

I drive in from Half Lake, where I live and work as a payroll clerk for a dental office. Sometimes I drive around town at one a.m. but during the daytime I shop at the local grocery store. I pay more money than if I were to just shop at the Walmart in Half Lake but I like the meat from here better. And if my money can help this little town's economy, I guess that's good.

When I come during the day, the parking lot is more than half filled with cars. Not all are local. I can tell just by looking at the paint jobs. If there's no rust, or if it has a full grille on the front, or has never been broken into, then it probably doesn't belong to Geshig. The closest reputable car dealership is thirty miles away, and on the high side of budgets that this town can't support except for some of the only good-paying jobs with the reservation.

On the Friday when I cash my check at the grocery store and buy a few small bags of food, there is a woman and her daughter sitting on the sidewalk out front. It's a hot day in early June but they don't appear bothered by the heat. They have a cardboard box with five puppies and a bowl of water inside. Three are brown with white underbellies and legs. Two are black and gray. All are staring up and out of the box, yipping for attention. No more than two months old.

On the side of the box in thick black marker is the word *Free*.

"You want one?" the woman says. She's a lithe Ojibwe woman with a bubbly olive face and long, swamp-tea hair. Her daughter is focused only on another pup, in her lap with a collar on. It's brindled, but with a white underbelly and piercing blue eyes.

"Oh I don't know …" I mumble, though I know instantly that I want one.

"Can't argue with free," she says. "You got a cigarette?"

"I don't." I walk away from them and then, without thinking, I turn back. "What kind do you smoke?"

"Marlboro Lights."

"Okay."

I buy a pack of cigarettes for the woman. "This for the brindle."

She lets out a surprised, satisfied laugh. "Damn, deal, guy!" There was no hesitation.

I pick up the other brindle from the box and get a good look. Male. Not shy. He licks my face as soon as he can and doesn't stop until I pull him away. The little girl is sad to see him go. "I'm Marion. What's your name?"

She has the same face as her mother, except with a wider smile, with big, bright teeth. "Ma'iinganikwezens! Mommy calls me Maya."

Ma'iinganikwezens. Wolf Girl. I smile. "That's a great name. And how about you?"

"Gerly."

"Gertie?"

"*Gerly.* Short for Gertrude." She blows her first puff of smoke to her right, as if that will protect her daughter's lungs. "Pokegama. I know. White-lady name. I always hated it."

The name seems familiar to me, but I don't think I recognize her face. "I know how you feel. 'Marion' got made fun of a lot growing up. Also didn't help that 'Lafournier' was easily made into 'La-Four-Eyes.'"

Gerly shakes my hand. "Good luck with the pup. He's a rezdog."

I have a name picked out for the dog before I leave the city limits. Basil. Because the herb was on sale in the store, two for one, but I only needed one. Now I have the other.

———

THE LIGHT ON THE message screen pings. The profile is blank but in a small town that could mean many things. Discretion. Shame. Desperation. The need for relief in a failing marriage. This man on the other end doesn't say much about what he wants. He won't even send a face pic and he doesn't want to see mine. I'm not closeted; I used to have my face showing but men wouldn't reply when they saw my Indian skin.

After hearing a brief description of my body, the only thing he will agree to is meeting at a dark place in the middle of the night. To most men this is probably a red flag.

Basil is sleeping in his pen near my TV and has food and water. He'll be okay for the next hour or two.

Right at the south end of Geshig, there is a rest area near a small park and a few acres of marshland. Until a few years ago, the park was an aging, dangerous structure filled with slivers, metal bars, and, according to some rumors, dried blood where children were either murdered or simply scraped their skin. Now it's a plastic pastel paradise with padded corners and a soft mulch ground instead of the pebbles that were once the endless ammo for rock fights. But most kids still prefer the elementary school park because of how much bigger it is.

The parking lot is well lit from the streetlights, and the new playground catches enough of it to discourage post-curfew children or drug deals.

Far behind the rest area building, away from the light pollution and near the cattails is where I meet him. As soon as I see his silhouette approach from another far end of the area, I begin my typical bout of last-minute nervousness and convince myself that he is a murderer. He is coming here to strangle me and throw me into the marsh. My body will not rot and future generations will study my mud-mummified corpse during their wetlands section of general science. That will be my reward for anonymous sex.

He sits next to me in the grass. "Hi." We sit there for a few moments before he reaches over to me. I expect his hand to land right at my groin, but instead he touches my stomach. His hand traces my sternum up to my shirt collar and then brushes over my neck and chin. For a long time, he touches the stubble on my face and says nothing. Then he moves back to my chest, lifting up my shirt and running each finger through the short tangles.

He removes my shirt and with both hands begins to squeeze my pecs, softly at first and then harder. I haven't experienced this before. Is this how a woman feels?

His hands dig into my skin. I let out a squeal and he stops. "Sorry! Sorry! I didn't mean to ..."

Even in a quiet whisper in the night, I recognize his voice. I smile and bring his hands back to me. "Don't worry. I liked it."

He lets out a breath that sounds like a smile and begins grabbing me again. "Can I kiss you?"

"Yes."

"I wanna see you first."

The outline of his head looks over to the parking lot before standing up. He caresses my hand and leads me toward the back of the rest area.

I see his face before he sees mine.

The moment Shannon recognizes who he's been groping in the dark, he pulls his hand away and runs back to the shadows of the grass.

"I knew I shouldn't have done this. I'm so fucking stupid!" His whispers are full of anger, almost enough to scare me. I follow him and repeat "Calm down" until he sits back on the grass and puts his head in his hands.

"Good to see you?" I pull my shirt back on and zip up my jeans.

"I shouldn't be here …"

"But you are here." I scoot closer a few inches. "Might as well make the best of it."

"Sorry. I don't think I can."

I laugh. "How were you having a better time feeling up a guy you didn't know?"

"You won't get it."

"I won't ask you to keep going but you had a need. You're here. I'm here. It's up to you."

"Do you have anything to drink? Whiskey? Beer?"

"At a rest area in the middle of the night? No, I don't. I have weed in my car though."

"No, I don't smoke. Can we go back to your place?"

It's a nice surprise to hear those words. Usually the men who meet in the dark would never want to have any contact outside of the shadows.

"If you want."

He lets out a loud sigh and falls back on the grass. "Or maybe we could go for a walk first?"

"I guess it's as good a time as any. Where to?"

Shannon Harstad was voted king at our junior prom. The theme was Fairy Tales and he danced with the queen, Leah Littlebear. I was working the concession stand, not actually part of the fun. Shannon's own participation was reluctant. He was never the spotlight kind of person, not like the other popular boys.

Without looking at me much, Shannon leads me across the

highway and onto the sidewalk off Fourth Street. Every time I try to catch up, his shoulders go tense and he walks faster.

"Have a place in mind?" I ask.

"Don't know."

"It's past the curfew."

"We're adults."

We walk past the Geshig Elementary School and just as we're about to pass the park, he stops. His gaze is transfixed into the darkness of the wooden fences and metal slides.

"Here."

At the edge of the fence we stand and look at each other's silhouettes. I didn't get a good look at him on the way here, even with the streetlights around, but I recognize the outline of his face. Even with age, he's still the same Shannon Harstad that I grew up with all through school.

"So ... you're gay?" He turns from me and starts walking away from the fence. "Wait, I'm sorry."

At first it seems he is angry but then he leads me toward another dark shape, about fifty yards from the park.

The merry-go-round.

He stops at the edge, but doesn't turn it. "Do you remember this thing? No one liked it because of the dog thing."

"I remember."

Every child in the elementary school knew the story. A dog went under the merry-go-round to die and no one would play on it. There was one time, though, a guy dared me to. The same guy I'm now hooking up with in the dark.

"Do you know if that was true or not?"

"No clue ..."

He turns to me and finally starts kissing me again. His hands grip my shoulders and he tries to lay me down on the merry-go-round.

"Um, bad idea," I say, pulling away from his tongue.

"Why?"

I push the iron bars and a loud, rusty screech blasts into the night. "Too loud. And we're way too close to a school. What if we get caught?"

He sighs and his lips brush mine just a little. "You're right. I'll take that drink now."

His truck follows my car through Geshig and westward toward Half Lake.

The first chance I had to move out of Geshig and off the Languille Lake reservation, I took it. I moved to the Twin Cities for college. And then as a few years passed, and after a disastrous relationship or two, I found myself back in Half Lake, and spending a lot of time in my hometown. It pulls me back here like the door at the end of a dream that you don't want to go through, but you can't control your feet.

My house is just on the inside of the Half Lake city limits, close to the highway. It's a small, pale cream house with a decent yard, and rent to own, so I'll be here for the foreseeable future.

Inside, I grab a bottle of whiskey and bring it to Shannon. He sits on my couch and I sit across from him in a small armchair. I would sit next to him but it's probably best to let him get a few drinks before we start again.

"I'm guessing you're not out?"

The bottle is thrown back. Eyes wince. "Fuck no."

"You're twenty-seven, right?"

"Exactly," he says with a bitter whiskey laugh. "I'm almost thirty. No wife. No kids. No fucking anything." He takes another drink and then stands up. "You're hard."

He's right. I had thought about being polite and hiding the bulge but I didn't think it would matter since whatever else he was feeling his lust is what got him in this situation.

"I have patient boners."

He walks over to me and grips it through my jeans. It's not an uncomfortable grip, but it feels unsexual. "What if I squeezed really hard? Would you like that? Would you still wanna fuck?"

I have no response but a hope that he doesn't deliver on that offer. I don't want that. And I don't know him, not anymore, probably not ever. I have no idea if saying the wrong thing will set him off and make this whole thing end badly. "Is that what you'd like to do?"

The grip relents a little and he traces the tip with his index finger. "Do you have a bed?"

"Of course I have a bed."

His hand stops. "Never done it on a bed before."

My first instinct is to laugh but instead, I stand up and lead him to my bedroom. The overhead light is off but there is a dull blue glow from the muted TV in the corner. Nearby in a pen is where Basil is sleeping. I sit at the edge of the bed and look up at Shannon. In the dusky light standing over me, he looks more imposing than ever. He has a round face and a shaved head, but his short beard looks thicker, bushier. The glare from the screen reflects in his glasses so I can't see his eyes.

"So ..."

Shannon wastes no time. I feel his hands grab my shoulders

and push me down. His body, softer than in high school but no less powerful, covers me. The taste of the whiskey hits my tongue. He smells sweet, fruity, almost like a car air freshener or a candle. The smell is soft, but his body is urgent, wanting.

Urgency doesn't equal grace, and it shows in the awkward, inexperienced way he positions my body and prepares to enter me. He avoids touching my ass with his hands, which does not make lubing an easy task for me with him on top. When the condom is on, he works himself inside slowly, asking over and over if I'm okay. As soon as I grab him by the hips and pull him in faster, his concern and gentleness are gone, and his body begins to take mine.

I lose myself in the fucking and when he finishes his last thrust, I'm not sure how much time has passed. He stays inside and on top of me for a few moments before pulling out and lying down next to me. We speak only with heavy breaths and light touches across our chests.

Though I enjoy myself during the entire encounter, I can't help but feel that his excitement, his moans of pleasure, his climactic roar, were not really for me.

He sits at the edge of the bed and stares down. "Cute pup."

"He's a little shit."

"Have you trained him?"

"Every day. But he chews things."

"Then you're not training him. He your only one?"

"Yeah ... Gonna take off now?"

"Unless you want me to stay."

I reach over and rub my hand across his side where his once-toned obliques have turned into soft, lightly haired love handles. "I want what you want. Plus, you drank half that bottle. Shouldn't drive."

"You have no clue how much I drink, do you?"

"Well, I do now." My hand moves to his thigh. "Next time I'll return the favor."

Shannon turns back to me. The screen is behind him, so his face is a silhouette that I can't read. But I think I saw a shadowed smile. "My phone alarm goes off at five a.m. And you're little spoon."

He wraps himself around me again and says no more.

⸻

IN THE MORNING, SHANNON doesn't explain what had bothered him so much when he realized who he was kissing in the grass. He doesn't say anything as he leaves, no forced small talk about meeting again, no awkward goodbye kiss. One moment I was sleeping against a warm, slick body, and then his alarm made him vanish into the still moist air.

I send him a message on the app that first connected us and thank him for his time. The light is no longer active.

Basil's bed is empty. I step carefully into the living room hoping the little guy hasn't pissed or shit on the floor. I find him in the kitchen eating, his bowl filled to the brim. It looks like a splash of milk is at the bottom of the brown pellets. Shannon must have done it before he left.

It's a lazy Saturday and I pass time by training Basil with small chunks of off-brand hot dogs, failing over and over to get "lay down" to stick. My neighborhood is not the best for walking, so I drive back to Geshig. Basil loves car rides, so he can't stop jumping from the front and back seats.

While walking him, I run into Gerly again. This time she isn't smoking.

"Hey!" She kneels to pet him and he greets her just as enthusiastically as the last time they were together. "How's the rezdog?"

"Learning. Slowly. Would you like to join us?"

"Uh, sure. I have some time. Wanna go to the Red Pine Diner?"

The diner is about as small-town stereotypical as you can think of, except instead of white housewives and truckers there are Indian mothers, on welfare or with full-time jobs. Either way, they are often the sole providers for their children. I know from experience with my mother.

Gerly orders for the both of us, insistent that I need to try the frybread/omelet combo. And she talks way more than I'm used to, almost like the pep rally girls back in high school. It turns out she is on the Geshig Elementary PTA, got her spot easily. She lives right in town. Runs a day care. Volunteers at many school events. Adored by the town mothers. If I was half as perfect for this town as she is, I would not still be here.

"So, is Maya's father in the picture?"

"No." She takes a small bite of frybread and eggs. "He died about twelve years ago."

Some quick mental math almost makes me spit out my food. "Oh! Kayden?"

The realization stuns me, where I knew Gerly's name from. Why hadn't I remembered that? Kayden and Gertrude had a daughter. I knew that, but I never knew the girl's name.

"Oh—I—wow, it's been that long already." Maya is only

eleven and she's spent her entire life with a murdered father. I have no idea what to say now.

"God, feels like yesterday sometimes," Gerly says. "You remember all that?"

How could I not? For Geshig, it was a "where were you?" kind of moment. The town, for those few years, existed as pre– and post–Kayden Kelliher. I was thirteen, less than a month left of eighth grade, sitting in my room listening to *Souvlaki* and staring at the walls. I remember because that's the only thing I did on school nights, listen to my mother's stoner records.

Instead of saying that, I just purse my lips, nod, and look at my hands. Much to my relief I find some words. "My mom used to babysit him when he was a kid. She cried. Wouldn't let me out of the house for months after."

"Geshig used to be so ghetto. Not anymore. We don't put up with that shit," Gerly says. "We chased out all the savs like you to Half Lake."

The fact that she is joking about this assures me that it's okay to laugh. "Yeah, we have our fair share of shady people."

She moves us effortlessly into another subject, not exactly an avoidance of the subject. Almost like boredom, as if her grieving for Kayden is completely behind her.

Her latest project is about the elementary school park that has fallen into disrepair.

"We finally got funding for a remodel."

"Gonna tear it down and start over or just like repaint it?"

"It's an iconic part of the town. Can't just tear it down."

Geshig's elementary park is modeled after a log cabin. The perimeter is almost a perfect square and the structures are layered wood with plenty of opportunities for splinters. On each corner of the perimeter there is a small totem pole—tall to children—that faces one of the cardinal directions. The eagle faces north. The bear, south. Fish, west; wolf, east. There is no meaning to the icons.

"Lots of good memories there."

"Lots of safety hazards." Gerly laughs. "We're gonna keep as much as we can. But for sure we're gonna get rid of the merry-go-round and replace it with a maze."

"Oh … That sounds fun."

"Remember when all the older kids talked about the dead dog underneath it?"

I smile and dig at the eggs with my fork. "Yep."

"I looked under it the other day. Guess what I saw?"

"Dirt?"

"Nothing but an empty 40-ounce."

"Classy. No dog bones?"

"Not a trace. I bet they just made that shit up."

"Maybe. All rumors have to start somewhere." I break off a small piece of frybread and slip it to Basil. His puppy teeth can barely chew it.

———

IT TAKES A FEW weeks, but Shannon is finally online again and horny for me.

Or perhaps not me but a body he can explore. A guy who has no reservations about letting him touch every in and out, any way he wants. He nearly wears me out by the end of that session. He stays all night, leaves for work, and comes right back to my place in the afternoon. At first he claims it's to see Basil but soon enough I'm on my stomach and back again and again.

I am not naive about men. I know this isn't him growing attached to me. It's some kind of reaction, but I'm not sure just what kind until he asks, "Promise not to tell anyone?" while lying on my chest.

"I promise."

"I fuck around with my roommate."

"Oh? How often?"

"Not like a lot but a few times every couple of months."

It doesn't dawn on me right away until I remember who he lives with.

"Tim? You sleep with Tim? Timothy Selkirk?"

"Yeah."

"Is it good?"

"No." He runs a hand down my stomach. Gentle, but I can't help remembering what he tried to do when we first hooked up. "You're better at it."

"Crazy odds. That three of us turned out gay."

Shannon's chest slowly pulses against mine as he lets out a few bitter laughs. "No, you're gay. Tim is straight. I date women. I just do this because . . . I don't fuckin' know, but I'm straight."

Not too uncommon, hearing dudes who love dick say they're straight. Mostly I believe them but after hearing this, I feel the need to press Shannon for more information.

"How did it start then? Someone had to have wanted it."

"Yep," Shannon says. "I did, but he kind of got the ball rolling." He pulls away from me and then tells the story. A normal day. Shannon thought he was alone in the house, started masturbating, and then Tim walked in on him. Shannon figured it would just be a slightly uncomfortable but humorous situation that they'd move past.

"Wrong. Kind of. We didn't laugh. We didn't move past it. And it was very uncomfortable."

Tim had walked right over to Shannon and grabbed his roommate's erection. He stroked it. At first it was slow and just hard enough to feel great, but Shannon surmises that as soon as he showed the slightest bit of pleasure on his face, Tim changed.

"Roughest hand job ever. I couldn't finish like that so . . . so he fucked me."

There is silence between us then. Tim was the tallest kid in our high school. Football and wrestling champion. And known for his anger issues.

"You—you wanted it, right?" I ask.

Minutes pass. He has nothing else to say about his relationship with Tim, and I'm filled with questions I'm too scared to ask. Even though Shannon is pressed against me, I can't stop thinking about what he's told me. Maybe Shannon senses this by how mechanical the motion of my hand rubbing his shoulder has become.

He gets up to leave. This time he manages a goodbye kiss and promises to text "soon."

I stare at my phone and wonder what soon means to a closeted former high school star.

———

EVEN A HIGHWAY CAN'T keep Geshig awake. I drive to the town at nearly three a.m., park my car at the grocery store, and watch a few cars pass by. Then I drive to the south end of town and park near the train tracks. Then I park outside the elementary school playground. From my window I can see the merry-go-round, doomed to be replaced, forgotten, just like the rumor.

I open the door and step into the black grass.

In high school, Shannon was the prom king. And Tim, he was the star quarterback. They were easily the most popular guys in our class, and as we neared the end, in the whole school.

I was there too, but I watched from the shadows in the crowd of the other, less talented children. From kindergarten onward, I tried to stay away from attention unless forced.

I stand in front of the merry-go-round and stare at the metal.

Shannon and I both lived on the same bus route. I never realized how much I watched him until he wasn't there. In seventh grade his seat was empty in the afternoon for a full week.

"Joined football?" I asked him one morning. My voice barely escaped under the confines of the jacket hood that draped over my face.

"Yeah." He sat up straight and grabbed on to the seat in front of him. "Took my dad years to convince my mom to let me. Now that I'm older she's not stopping me."

"Seems like it will hurt. That what she's scared of?"

"Yeah and that's why we play. We're guys. We live to get hurt."

"By time you get home it's gonna be dark out."

"We practice outside."

"Do you think you'll be good at it?"

"I hope so. The coaches begged me to join."

"They asked me too. I don't know why. Never said I wanted to."

"We need all the dudes we can get. Even the skinny ones."

He reached over and pinched my collarbone. Not painfully, but rough enough to jerk my reflexes and make me pull away. "Ow! Stop! I don't know how to play. And I'm not strong."

"If you came to hell week we woulda cured you of that right away."

I shrug. "Maybe next year."

That was a lie. It was a lie when I said it and it was a lie the next five years when I didn't join any other groups. Shannon kept at it each season after, and by the time he hit junior year our football team won state. But for all that success, he was more like me when it came to attention. He wasn't a glory hog or a show-boater. He gladly let the more rowdy and wild guys on the team be the center of attention.

And me, through it all, I just watched him until the ride ended and I left Geshig. Still don't really know why I came back or why I'm still here.

I grab the rusty bar of the merry-go-round and push as hard as I can. The screech of the rust cuts into my ears and the silent town. The bars circle faster and faster until the structure is spinning as fast as it can manage.

No one played on this when we were kids except me and Shannon. Must have been third or fourth grade. He dared me to do it. I sat on the cast-iron platform, held on to the rust-brown bars, and he pushed.

When he had it spinning fast enough, he jumped on across from me and held on tight. We tipped our heads back, laughed, and on the count of three we let go and tumbled into the grass. My eyes jerked back and forth, but I managed to crawl over to him. He was staring underneath the iron. We inched forward, closer, closer, until Shannon screamed and drove his finger into my chest. We got up and ran away laughing.

The memory is burned into my mind, and it still burns hot now. Warm lines run down my face and drip onto the cast iron. Shannon will never be with me the way I'd like, but he'd always be here with me, laughing, spinning.

When I hear the thumping, I stop pushing the bars and let the turning slow to a halt. There is a low whimpering that turns to panting. A train passes through the south side of town, its horn louder than a rusty playground could ever be, and a tawny mutt crawls out from underneath the metal.

In the dark I can't tell what kind of dog it is. Part German shepherd, part pit bull, part wolf. Probably at least one part ghost.

"Hey, boy. You wanna play? You wanna go for a run? Let's go for a run!"

The dog jumps into my arms and knocks me to the ground. He slobbers all over my face and then begins to circle me. He crouches, butt in the air, waiting for me. "Let's go."

I run with him all around the field, circling the merry-go-round, and eventually circling the park. He runs with a lopsided gait but he is faster than any dog I've ever seen. Two more times he tackles me to the ground and licks my face. He has newborn-puppy breath, like Basil.

My breath soon becomes labored puffs and when I stop to rest, the dog disappears into the darkness of the sleeping town.

He had no collar. No name. No owner. Just a rumor.

IN THE WEEKS SINCE I picked him up from the box marked *Free*, Basil has grown quickly. He sheds fur all over my house and still chews on errant objects when I'm not looking. He no longer sleeps in the pen on the floor. He is just big enough to jump onto my bed. Sometimes he kicks me in the face, either by accident or to wake me up for food or walks.

Hey...you wanna?

The message is from Shannon, this time a text message and not through an app.

It's been weeks. That's how you ask?

Yes.

Come over then.

He knocks on my door a half hour later and we walk right to my bed. I'm rock hard and ready to go when he kisses me, but he stops and begins to pet Basil.

"Hey you. How's my buddy? You got so big!"

"So, how's it going?" I ask as I wait.

"Okay. Tim might move out soon. Not sure if I'm going to find a new roommate or find another place."

Before I can talk about his roommate again, he distracts me with his mouth.

I expect him to leave as soon as he's had his fill but he stays. He suggests we go for a walk in the neighborhood with Basil. As we're walking, I notice that he always tries to keep the dog between us and takes a step to the side if we get too close.

Basil doesn't pay attention to us. He just leads us through the streets and doesn't care where we end up.

"What have you been up to?" he asks.

Resurrecting dogs. "Nothing. Just work and stuff. You?"

"Same. It's the busy season but come fall it'll slow way down. What do you do again?"

"Payroll and accounting."

"For a hospital, right?"

"Sort of. Dental office."

"Right. How has that been?"

We have had this conversation before. Each time I tell him the small-talk details of my life he's barely attentive. This time seems no different, but he looks at me more when I speak.

"The dentist office is okay. Tedious and boring but pays the bills."

"Is it depressing?"

"What do you mean?"

"Just seeing so many names and numbers," Shannon says. "When I'm cleaning out a cabin at the resort and people leave their trash behind I guess I think about what kind of people they are and what they're doing. Why they chose Nine Isle to stay at. I don't know. Maybe it's not the same."

I kick a small rock in front of me and Basil's ears perk up as he watches it. He sniffs at it when it stops rolling and then moves on.

"It's not a big deal," Shannon says. "Sometimes I just think too much."

"I know the feeling. Hard to stop."

"What do you think about too much?"

I stop walking and stare at Basil's neck as he pants. "Just regrets, I guess."

What I think about is my first boyfriend, Gordon. I think

about the last day I went to his place. The last time we hooked up, and how I left feeling ashamed and dirty, and how I wished I would've stayed there overnight and maybe we'd still be together.

But Shannon keeps claiming he's straight, and I don't think he'd understand this, so I say nothing.

We make a loop around a few blocks and then go back to my house. I stop at the sidewalk and look up at him. He's changed a lot since high school. The hint of a receding hairline makes him keep it all shaved except for on his chin, lips, and neck. He's thicker, like most men get, but no less muscular. And his eyes are almost constantly bored unless he's on top of me.

"Take care, bud." He kneels and pets Basil on the head. "I'm gonna head back home now."

He gives me a faint, dark smile in the evening light and hesitates. Is this a cue? I think so. I step forward, rise slightly on my toes, and lean in to kiss him. He loses the smile and takes a few quick breaths. My lips land. He lets it happen, tongue and all, for just a moment before breaking away and turning to leave. I look around as he gets in his truck and drives away.

It's dusk. No one is watching, no one saw.

I bring Basil inside, sit down on my bed, and text Shannon: *I'm sorry if that scared you.*

I stare at the phone's tiny screen and wait.

===

SOMETIME IN THE NIGHT, I lie awake and stare at Basil, but instead of my loving mutt I can only see that thing that crawled out from the darkness. It's then that the memory comes back clear.

It was third or fourth grade. Shannon and I stood at the edge of the playground and stared at the metal in the distance.

"Let's go play on it," he said.

"What about the zombie dog?"

"That's a lie the older kids made up."

"It's metal. What if we get hurt?"

He grabbed my wrist and pulled me with him. Hard enough to leave a bruise. "We're boys. That's what we're supposed to do."

Two

Nine Isle

LEFT HIM BACK THERE, didn't you? Didn't give him the kiss goodbye he wanted.

But why care?

You're a man's man. You're not a faggot. You don't fuck with guys.

=====

THE RESORT RUNS THE same every year, no matter what part of the country the tourists come from. The majority are southern Minnesotans, but sometimes there's a family from out of state or even out of the country. They all do the same things, buy the same campfire food from the Geshig store, rent the same canoes or paddleboards, camp in the same cabins or tent sites that thousands have before them.

You should've left Geshig when you had the chance. Dad said so back in high school when you wanted to get your first job cleaning cabins.

"Don't waste your time around here, son," he warned. "A

part-time job becomes a full-time pretty quick in this town and before you know it you'll be forty and wishing you left this reservation."

"It's just some extra cash in the summer. I didn't sign a contract for life or something."

But you did. When your sweat dripped across Lake Anders and the small chain of nine islands that gave the resort its name, when you worked longer hours to pay for that truck for senior year, when you were too busy worrying about which girls were next on the list, you signed the contract without knowing.

You cast a line and got snagged, not that that's a bad thing.

No need to worry about the DNR's permits since the resort covers you for that, so you and Dad can fish whenever and park the boat at half the fee.

Right now, you need to fish. Get out on the waters and cleanse. Release. There's nothing better than catching, cleaning, and eating a walleye or a northern and knowing it was done by your own hands.

Because you're a north woods man, you don't do shit with guys.

———

DAD NEVER TALKS ABOUT his health, but you've noticed he's been struggling when he gets into the boat for a few months now. But you haven't brought it up to him. Instead you say things like…

"Doing okay over there?"

"Yeah, just kinda tired, ya know? I been waking up in the middle of the night cause of this dang heat."

"Gotcha." Behind his back you smile to yourself about his thick Minnesotan accent and thank god that he didn't pass it down, or so Mom says. She came from Fargo, but spoke like a woman from the Deep South, and the mix of the two growing up along with the reservation kids in school somehow allowed you to have a regular voice. Talk normal, just like you should.

The boat speeds out onto Lake Anders, smooth as a canoe, quick as a car. Another benefit of working for Nine Isle. Boats are expensive as shit, but the boss gets good financing deals.

Out on the lake is where a man finally relaxes. No more gritting teeth and breathing out the nose. Men belong on the water.

On the first cast, the line gets caught on another. Dad doesn't watch the water like he used to. Both of you have won a lot of fishing contests, but age wins all.

"What whatchur doing, Shanno!" he says, not a glance over. "I taught you better than that."

He did teach you better but there's too much distraction, too many text messages.

"Sorry, Dad."

The lines are easy to untangle and soon they are trolling through Anders for muskie and walleye. Here they grow biggest in the state, and the lake doesn't even have that distinction, though it is large, and every inch of the shore is instinct, familiar.

The wind blows from the south today, and it drags the boat across the waters despite the cinder-block anchor being dropped. Only small perch bite for the next few hours, the stubborn waves warning the prize fish of the surface dangers.

But there's no giving up. You're the fisherman Dad taught you to be.

The cell phone vibrates against your thigh and invades the peace of the windy lake. The messages come in one after another like useless eelpout.

"New girlfriend?" Dad asks, nudges his elbow against your chest.

"Yeah. Bitches are annoying."

Fags are annoying too, but you wouldn't know anything about that.

"Oh I'm sure they're not all bad. Your ma and I'd love for you to bring someone home one day."

"I've brought girls home, Dad. Ma never likes them."

"She gets that from your grandma. She never liked me none either, but she warmed up. Just give her time, and she'll love whoever you bring home."

"Thanks."

At the end of the day, there are no muskies or walleye in the cooler, but Dad smiles anyway. Nothing disappoints him. Only one thing could ever disappoint him.

———

THE MESSAGES DON'T STOP at night. They come in uninvited, some of them angry, some desperate, some with naked pictures.

Stop messaging me, Marion.

No. You're being ridiculous.

I don't know what you're talking about, bro. I don't even fuck with guys. GOODBYE!!

Falling asleep brings no relief, the only thing you see is him.

You don't know how it happens, you never know. One moment he's not on your mind, the next you're already in your truck, on the way to his house, and inside his bedroom before you can remember the regret that swells through your mind every time you leave.

Every damn time.

"Hey."

His voice, soft, like a woman's, it scares you. Freezes you in place. You don't know what to do or how to respond so you fall onto your stomach, bury your face in the mattress, and somewhere between the beginning, the end, the climax, pain and pleasure, postcoital regret, you think you feel something like happiness.

Marion stares at the door. He knows you want to leave, because you always do.

Before you turn to the pile of clothes on the floor, you look at his shirtless body. Small lines of hair, a jungle compared to most Indian men you've seen, and maybe just for a moment you think that it looks like a nice place to rest.

His hands run through your moss-short hair and beard while you listen to his heartbeat, right below your ear. Nothing needs to be said, nothing at all.

"When was your first time?" you whisper.

He lets out a breathy laugh that you can feel brush past your face. "I was nineteen. Living in the cities. Had my first . . . boyfriend, I guess."

"Did you top or bottom?"

He laughs again. "I don't remember . . . Sometimes I try not to."

You roll over, so you can see him but still feel his body on your head and back. "Why?"

"It's complicated," he says. "I was ... well, like you are now. Didn't want anyone to know what I did, even if it was in private. So I stopped seeing him."

"What was his name?"

"Gordon."

"Do you still talk?"

"No."

His hands stop caressing your scalp and you fall asleep, each beat of his heart a lullaby.

———

BEZHIG. ONE.

You're straight. You only fuck with dudes when you're drunk, but that's just the whiskey.

Not all nine of the islands are habitable by humans. Three are too small, only six are used as campgrounds, and the biggest one is half owned by rich snowbirds who only show up for weeks in the summer. One island has a boys' summer camp, also for the rich, but there is enough space on each for public camping.

The islands are named after the Ojibwe words for *one* through *nine*, but you've never been good at speaking it.

Bezhig. One.

The first island is the biggest. In that way, the islands go in reverse order with the last three being the ones that men can't really do anything with, unless they wanna camp on ten square feet of prickly grass and wake up in the water. What makes Bezhig notable is the presence of a small lake, a record holder for a lake-within-a-lake, but it's been disputed because of its size.

Niizh. Two.

The second largest, and the only one not owned fully by the state. The land is open to the public, which of course means the rich. No resorts on Niizh, just private summer lake homes and thick woods. Marion was quick to point out that none of the owners were Indians. He's always looking for problems.

Niswi. Three.

The third island is the most likely destination for campers who aren't rich, with its smaller size being cheaper to rent but more crowded.

Niiwin. Four.

Marion says the way they're spelled on the signs is wrong but Indians didn't develop their language for English.

Naanan. Five.

You don't fuck with guys.

Ingodwaaswi. Six.

Ignoring him has been fruitless. It's more than a hint of disinterest, it's a clear answer that he won't accept ... Still, it's nice to be wanted.

Niizhwashwi. Seven.

One more message and you'll kick his ass.

Nishwaashwi. Eight.

You like women, drinking, fishing, hunting.

Zhaangaswi. Nine.

If Dad knew, he'd kill you or keel over. Either way, there would be death.

Midaaswi. Ten.

There's no tenth island. But Marion taught you how to say

ten, back in middle school when you were struggling in class. He was always a good guy, you know that.

Bezhig.

You want him, but you're just not that kind of man.

———————

THE BOSS CALLS AT seven a.m.

"Shannon, we need ya ta clean up da west shore."

"Clean up what?"

"Dead rabbits."

"The fuck?"

"Sumfins' been killin' critters around the Tamarack Walk. Tourists don't like to see dead bodies on their vacations. You get to scoop up the guts."

"Lucky me. Any idea what it is?"

"Nah, but bring a gun just in case."

Driving from the east parking lot over to the rest area, you're sure to keep your eyes away from the grass. The trail begins about a half mile from the rest area, over a bridge that the Mississippi passes under, and today there are few people hiking. Your nose guides you, and you find the first carcass only a mile in.

The tan and white spots on what little fur is left are familiar. A fawn or a doe, hacked to bits. Not the graceful cuts Dad taught you how to do, just a violent mess. The carrion smell is thick, but you're used to it. The fetid mush falls into the sack like a colostomy bag and the search for more begins.

From the first pile of guts, it's not hard to track the rest. They are spread out like a vicious connect-the-dots. The worst is a carcass that looks like a cat. It is no bigger than a human forearm, each bone like a toothpick. Almost all bone except for a few patches of flesh and fur still attached, nothing that tells what kind of critter the mush used to be.

When all the bodies are bagged, you dig a hole off the side of the trail and bury the stench where no one or thing will ever find it. The last scoops of soil that round out the top of the hole come with a satisfaction, a job well done.

Because you're a man's man. This is what you do.

Three

What Children Whisper

BASIL'S GROWTH SPURT ENDS just as September begins. He's about fifty pounds now, most of it muscle. He has short legs, thick arms, shoulders, and withers. His face is wide, squarish like a pug's, but with a long muzzle. Once big and floppy, his ears are now small points on a fat face, as if they've been the same size since his birth.

My tiny house and yard are no longer enough for him. Now he wants the world. I bring him to the Geshig Elementary School park. Right away, he takes an interest in the soil underneath the spot where the merry-go-round sat. His eyes grow big and focused as he paws at the dark circle.

"Think you can find it for me?" He pants and jumps on my leg. "Do your best."

He begins to walk and pull on his leash. Basil isn't a trained hunting hound. It's unlikely that he's leading me anywhere intentionally. But stranger things have happened in this park.

First he brings me through the park gates and to the foot of the biggest slide. On top it's a faded, metallic red with hundreds of scuff marks and a faint pattern of a brick chimney. On the other side it's covered in graffiti, mostly permanent marker that has been either scribbled over by more marker or scratched out with a file or knife.

A piece of graffiti etched into the eagle pillar catches my eyes, and brings back memories. It's an upside-down crucifix with the initials *NN* in the top corners. Neo-Nazi. Or Native Nazi. I don't remember what they called themselves but I was standing in the same place I am now when it was carved into the wood.

The summer right before eighth grade, me and Amos were walking around town trying to escape the heat and decided on the park. We went underneath the wooden walkway that was attached to the eagle pillar. The pebbles were cool on our skin and left behind a chalky residue.

Amos pulled out a small blue plastic pipe and began to light it. "You want a hit?"

"No."

"Sure?"

"Yes."

Amos smiled and took the hit. "It's cheap shit anyway. When you do smoke you should get some good grass."

"I'll keep that in mind."

"I wouldn't even smoke this stuff but I can't live without it like every day."

"Mmmhmm…"

"Where does your mom get hers?"

"I don't know." That was a lie. I knew where my mother bought her drugs, but it wasn't a place I wanted Amos to ever try to find. Though I never really thought of him as a guy that needed to be protected, I didn't want to have any part in letting Geshig claim him.

Before we left the park, Amos took out a pocketknife and began to carve the symbol of the gang that he claimed he and his older brother, Isaac, were a part of. I don't think they espoused any ideals close to those of the Nazis, I think they were just too young and naive to really consider how that name would come across. Then again, teenage gangs don't exactly have logic working in their favor.

Basil pulls me forward, away from the eagle pillar and toward the edge of the park and the highway.

Geshig's public high school was always more Indian than white, but even the white children were like a special kind of Reservation White. They knew the town. They knew powwows. They knew the culture. Some went to church, some didn't. If they had bad things to say about Indians, it was usually a joke, and even if it wasn't, the same things could easily be said back to them. But Amos, his family was not that kind of white.

They had moved to Geshig from southern Minnesota only three years before. At lunch, I saw a pale, blond kid with crooked teeth and tired eyes. He was sitting alone but didn't seem concerned about it at all.

I'd like to think that befriending him was the kind act of a fifth grader who saw the new kid sitting alone, but the only reason I sat down was because he happened to be at the table where I usually sat alone. I don't like breaking routines.

Basil takes me across the highway toward the north side of town. I'm not scared to go through there, but I prefer to avoid it if I can. *Ghetto, project, slum,* any word you can use to disparage a whole neighborhood is used to describe the north side. It's a place of cracker-box houses with few bedrooms and many people in each. The older members of the community sometimes call it the NeighborHUD.

Relief. When we reach the other side of the highway, Basil walks past the main road into the north side and toward the eastern exit of the town. Here the woods grow thicker and the air smells fishy from the lake wind.

"Why is there a cop here?"

It was not the response I expected when I had sat down and asked Amos his name. "Um. To protect us?"

"From what?"

"Bombs?"

"Who brought a bomb?"

My face turned red and I hoped no one had heard him. "There was some bomb threats or something. I wasn't in school when they happened but everyone was scared."

The bomb threat was like a mini-9/11 that I had slept through. My mother, Hazel, had made me stay home because of a fever and when I returned the teachers were tense, the kids quieter, and multiple cops were patrolling.

Amos glared in the direction of the school cop. "I don't like cops."

"Why not?"

"Because they're part of the government. And I don't like the government."

You and everyone else, my old friend.

"My mom doesn't either."

"Do you?"

My answer was honest back then and today. "I'm scared of them." Amos laughed at me and then told me his name.

My arm jerks forward and the leash almost slips out of my hand. Basil pulls hard enough to make the tug of the collar choke himself. He is staring down a paved trail that leads into the forest. The leaves are fading but still thick, and they hide everything behind them in green shadows.

Ahead is a long, winding trail called the Tamarack Walk. For nature lovers. Bikers. Kids playing hooky. And something that has captured Basil's full attention.

The first few yards of the trail are in flat land with the occasional mossy mound and felled log. After a while the ground begins to turn into small swamps filled with green beads and lily pads all over the surface. For the next few miles, the trail skirts the lake and most of the land will be wet and muddy.

Basil's intense focus lets up when he discovers the wilderness on the sides of the pavement. Every weed, fern, or rock that tumbles because of his own kick captures his short attention span. After he satisfies his curiosity, his focus shifts back to the distance of the trail and he pulls against the leash again.

The wind brings the scent of rotting fish from the lake and the branches of the tamaracks shake and chatter.

When me and Amos walked on this trail, he offered a joint but when I declined he didn't keep asking.

"No, that's totally legit, bro," he said. "My brother forced me to when I was like ten and now I can't stop."

"What an ass."

"Yeah he is. Lucky it wasn't meth or pills."

"Did you tell your mom?"

"Ha. No. She thinks Isaac is too much of an angel. Probably woulda just blamed me."

I still remember his voice having the hint of a drawl, as if his family was from much farther south than Faribault, Minnesota. When he moved up here the difference in accents was noticeable right off the bat and some of the other kids took to calling him hillbilly.

On that day, or one of the many times we walked that trail, we came across a golf cart with a full set of clubs. It was parked on the side of the pavement. No one was around.

"Hey man ..." Amos giggled. "You want a club?"

"I don't think I need one."

His hands shook and he kind of bobbed from one foot to the other. "You want one anyway? Think about it. They're just sitting here. We found them. I think I'm supposed to take them."

"Okay," I said. "Do it."

He grabbed the handle of one of the clubs and a woman's voice shouted from somewhere behind us. "What the hell are you kids doing?"

"Book it, Marion!" We ran away from the voice and deeper into the trail where there was nothing on either side but swamp and cattails. Neither of us was very fit but with the right motivation we managed to make a good distance before we stopped and caught our breath.

Amos couldn't stop smiling through his labored breaths. "I knew we were being watched. I could feel it!"

"Shut the hell up. No, you didn't." My legs collapsed and I tumbled to my back. "Why did you even try to grab it then?"

"For the rush. I love doing shit like this. Running from the cops and shit."

"You don't know if she was a cop."

"She was probably gonna call the cops though. Same thing."

I don't think there was any one moment when me and Amos drifted apart as friends. We just talked and hung out less and less until we just nodded to each other when we passed through the hallways. He didn't graduate. I didn't say goodbye when I moved out of Geshig.

A foul smell hits my nose. Basil is barking and whining. I look around for the source and find a tattered and rotting corpse of an animal. I can't tell what kind because few traces of it are left. Nothing but brownish fur, scattered bones, and globs of browning flesh. The collection would attract most dogs but Basil won't go near it.

We walk past the fetid mess only to find it's not the only one. Carrion litters this part of the trail like bread crumbs. And in the distance, I see what laid it.

The dog from under the merry-go-round.

With a red maw and wide eyes staring into mine. Basil barks and with a reinvigorated energy he pulls the leash right out of my hand and gives chase. The other dog turns and speeds off into the woods.

What else can I do but follow?

I don't have the speed or grace to follow two dogs. One is not quite fully grown and the other has been dead for almost two decades, but still they leave me far behind. The land isn't quite as swampy as before, and it gets drier the farther I run, but my boots and pant legs get covered in mud.

Unlike most people my age, I think I'm more fit in my mid-twenties than when I was a young teen. I can follow the distant noise of the dogs barking for what I guess to be about two miles.

I find Basil at the edge of a clearing in the trees, hunched and snarling. Inside the clearing are rows of tombstones and graves, some old, some new. The other dog stares at me, but now with sad eyes. It's standing over a grave.

Basil stays in place as I walk to the tombstone. I don't see where the other dog runs to because I can't stop staring at the name on the tombstone.

Kayden Kelliher.

Before I met Gerly last summer, his was a name I hadn't thought about in years. Maybe a whole decade. I never actually met him myself, but he was the kind of guy who knew everyone in the community.

Basil approaches with caution and doesn't lower his shoulders until I sit down at the foot of the grave.

"Hi, Kayden."

The gravestone is black marble with Kayden's face etched into the center. A blue ribbon with a faded gold medallion hangs around a small crystal cross with no markings.

"How's that basketball thing working out?" Silence, except for a few whimpers from Basil. He paces around the cemetery in circles and lets out pathetic barks at nothing.

"Basil, you got us here," I say. "You know what any of this is about?"

Basil barks into the distance, runs to the edge of the graveyard, and pisses on a fence.

SHANNON'S TRUCK IS QUIET as it comes into view. Basil and I are about a mile down the road from the cemetery. The other dog is nowhere to be found, and Basil can't or won't pick up the scent, if there really was one.

"Hey," Shannon says when he stops. Basil jumps into the back of the cab and I sit in the passenger seat.

"Thanks."

Shannon looks at my mud-caked boots and legs. "Um. Do you need to tell me something?"

"Never chase a dog through a swamp."

He looks back at Basil and sees the mud and detritus lining his fur.

"I see … But why were you over here in the first place?"

For a moment I consider telling him about the other dog, but remembering its bloody maw and eyes makes me want to forget about it entirely. "I was on the Tamarack Walk with the pup. He got loose and I had to chase him down."

"You sure?" His voice is low and monotone.

"Why wouldn't I be sure about that?"

"My job is a mile from here. Were you trying to see me?"

I sigh. "What if I said yes? Would you be okay with that?" He doesn't answer. "I was just out for a walk with Basil. He got loose and I had to chase him through the swamp."

"But why were you walking in Geshig instead of home?"

"Same reason as usual. I like it here."

His laugh is bitter as he pounds the steering wheel with his right hand. "I don't think anyone from here would believe that."

"Well, that's my only answer. But since we're apparently talking again, why haven't you been answering me?"

Only the sound of Basil panting passes between us. The truck pulls into town and he asks me where I want him to drop me off.

"The rest area." The silence becomes even more uncomfortable as he pulls into the parking lot and brings me to my car.

"I don't know what to tell you, Marion. I just don't."

I glance around the parking lot. No one is nearby, so I take the risk of scaring him further away and put my hand on his thigh. I can feel his body tighten, but he doesn't push my hand away. "I get it. I've done this before with other men. I get it."

Without another word I open the door, step outside, and don't look back in. Basil jumps out and tries to run off, but I make sure to wrap the leash around my hand this time.

"I can train him for you sometime," Shannon says. "You may be enrolled here but I know the rezdogs more than you."

One last smile between us. I shut the door and he leaves us behind.

━━━━━

I WOULD SAVE A lot of gas money if I stopped driving into Geshig, but I don't really worry about that. My job pays well enough and my car is good on gas mileage. Still, what a waste of money, right? What is in this town for me?

Right now, I'm walking past the corner of Fifth and Douglas to see a friend who has invited me over. It's a cream-colored house with colorful decorations all around the roof, walls, and yard. Wind chimes with small stained-glass panels. Paper lanterns with rainbow-colored ribbons. Various statues of Americana on the dried lawn.

A hand-painted sign by the mailbox that reads TWO SISTERS DAYCARE.

Gerly answers the door with an infant in her arms. "Hey, Marion! Just a minute."

She walks back inside for a moment and returns without the child. "Don't worry, he's my nephew. I don't have any other kids here right now." I follow her into the kitchen. The table and counters are cluttered but not unclean, and the air is filled with the smell of burned sage and sandalwood.

Her sister, Angie, walks in just as we sit down. She is a stout woman with mahogany skin, a tight ponytail, and long earrings made of purple and yellow beads. In her arms is the young boy, who stares around the room aimlessly. "This your new man?"

"Ish, shut up."

"Well, is he?"

"No. But he ain't yours either."

"So selfish …"

Gerly rolls her eyes and ignores her sister's presence. "So how you been, guy? How's the pup?"

"Getting too big. But he's not as bad as you said he'd be."

"Just wait. He'll destroy your house if you let him."

"No, he's too cute."

"Mmmhmm. Sure. How are things with that guy?"

Life is always strange, but beyond high school and college there is a bit of a polarity switch. To young eyes, the adult world is a mystery to be tackled but eventually most settle into how ordinary it all is. Something simple to children like making friends then becomes a daunting task. For me that's the opposite. It's not daunting now. I've told Gerly all about Shannon even though we've not hung out much.

"Oh, not great. Maybe sometimes," I say.

"Oh yeah?"

"It's nightmare and bliss depending on the day."

Angie catches on and can't hide her wide eyes and smile of realization. "Oh."

"I'm afraid I'd disappoint as you or your sister's 'new man.'"

Most don't know a proper reaction to learning my sexuality, at least in a casual manner. Some will insist how "cool they are with it" or say something like "good for you." Others, the ones who do it best, have no reaction and carry on the conversation. Angie's face has already passed the chance for the latter but she doesn't drift into the former much.

"That's why Gerly likes you. If a guy hits on her she bitches him out like he called her fat." She laughs and sets the toddler down on the floor, and immediately the child crawls about. "I'm probably too much for you anyway." Angie shimmies and shakes her breasts and stomach. Gerly laughs and pushes her sister on the shoulder.

"Oh get outta here, you horny bitch!"

As Angie stops laughing she looks back to me. Now it's my eyes that get caught reacting.

Without the child in her arms I can see the design clearly. It's a memorial shirt. *Gone but never forgotten.* A young man's image, smiling, next to his name and dates of birth and death.

Kayden Kelliher.

Angie and Gerly both stop their laughing. At first I worry

that I soured the mood but Gerly smiles and talks about how she and Angie founded their day care. "It was kind of my idea, kind of our ma's idea."

"I was tricked into it," Angie claims. "'It'll be a lot of money and working with kids will be fun!'"

Gerly also tells me more about her current project of remodeling the elementary school park.

As Gerly talks, I realize that Angie might know something about the dog. She's closer to my age than her older sister is. We would've been in the same class, but she transferred to the reservation-run school when she was thirteen.

"Angie," I say when a moment opens. "You went to Geshig Elementary, right?"

"Sure did."

"Do you remember there being any rumors about a dog under the merry-go-round?"

"Uh, kind of? I never played on it because they said it was haunted."

"Would you happen to remember who you first heard it from?"

"Fuck no! You crazy? That was like fifteen years ago!"

"I thought so."

We do not talk about Kayden or the dog again. Instead, Gerly once again fills me in on the adult world of the local school and her day-care business. Despite the clear-as-day reminder of Kayden on her sister's bosom, her voice is no different than when I met her. It has always been happy.

THE EAST END OF Geshig is not the same kind of eyesore that the northern slum is, but it's only better in looks. No matter what neighborhood, this town can't shed its skin.

Amos answers the door with a cigarette in his mouth. He is wearing a tattered and stained tank top and camo-patterned cargo shorts. "Come on in."

I walk in, sit down on his couch, and he lights a joint. "Sorry for the mess. The old lady brought the girls to see their grandma."

The apartment is no different than usual, just less crowded, but no matter how many times I tell him it's not a big deal he always apologizes.

We don't have a lot of deep conversations, only smoking and pricing. If it wasn't for him I doubt I'd smoke unless I'm with my mother because I'd be too nervous or awkward to try to meet another dealer.

When I feel the high creep into my chest and shoulders, I have the urge to break our usual routine and ask him a few questions.

Back in eighth grade, after Kayden Kelliher died, Amos claimed to know the identity of the real murderer. His own brother, Isaac. But there was no mystery about what happened. Everyone knew. Everyone at school whispered about what they thought really happened, but there was never any real question to be explored.

Amos, why did you claim your brother murdered Kayden Kelliher when everyone knew the truth? Did you hate your brother or do you know something others don't?

It would be that easy to speak the words but I know there's nothing there. Nothing but a middle school whisper.

There was no mystery surrounding the murder of Kayden Kelliher. But why did the playground Revenant lead me right to his grave?

Amos and I finish the joint without another word. I pay him for a few ounces and then stuff the baggie into my jacket pocket.

The highway is nothing but a blur when I drive. Bad habit I picked up from Hazel. When I return home, I pour myself a glass of whiskey and Coke and slam it down. I pour another and sip it slowly. It's Shannon's favorite whiskey, but I will be lucky if he ever comes back here to enjoy it.

Basil is sleeping on the couch but perks up when I tickle the top of his nose. I let him outside to relieve himself, thankful he has not done it in the house. That was only a problem for the first few weeks but eventually he learned.

Another glass of whiskey down. Did I drink like this before I reunited with Shannon this summer? I know he has been a heavy drinker for a while, but have I been any more stable?

I let Basil back inside and he joins me on the couch. He falls asleep with his head on my lap and I try to relax.

I look at my phone. It's beginning to blur and I need to squint my eyes hard to see the screen because somehow the depth of the glass has increased. Shannon hasn't texted back and right now seems as good a time as any to apologize. Again.

This time he replies within seconds. *I'm coming over.* Nothing more.

Awful as it is to say, the memory of Kayden Kelliher should not be important to me. I didn't really know him and he didn't know me. Aside from Gerly and Maya, who I just met in June, I don't know any of his relatives. All I really know of Kayden is the fact that he was killed.

For us kids, his death was just another source of rumors, something to tell each other when no one was listening. To the adults, he was their hero. He was the young man with potential, an Indian boy who would leave the reservation for bigger and better things. Even my mother had a place for him in her heart.

My eyes are still unfocused as I look at my phone but I manage to find my mother in my contacts list. I speak a few words out loud just to see if I can manage full sentences but my voice slops out like thick mustard so I send her a quick text.

Can I come see you soon?

Later, outside my window I see Shannon's truck park behind my car. Shannon walks inside without knocking. I drop my phone onto the couch and follow him into the bedroom.

Four

Ogichidaag (**Warriors**)

Gwiiwizensag (**Boys**)

"YOU DON'T THINK THEY'RE being too rough, do you?" Hazel asked.

"Boys will be boys," said Kayla. "They're okay."

The two women watched the group of children wrestle on the lawn. Five boys and one girl. "What about her?"

"Eh, she's a rez girl. She can handle herself."

Out on the grass, the young girl Nora wrestled a football away from Kayla's son, Kayden.

Circle of life, Kayla thought. Back when Kayla was their age, Nora's mother had always bested her in playground roughhousing. Kayden tried to wrestle the ball back from her but suddenly, from his side, another boy, Jared, slammed into him with his shoulder, like a bull.

Kayden fell hard. Without hesitation, he jumped up and tackled Jared. His small fists began to flail into Jared's face, and

Jared returned the fire. The group around them backed away and began to scream for help.

Hazel jumped to her feet, holding tight to her toddler, but Kayla calmly stood up and walked over to the commotion. "Don't worry, I got this."

Kayla pulled the boys apart by their arms and held them in place by their shirt sleeves. "That's enough. It's just a game, kids."

From across the park, another woman saw the scuffle and jogged over to Kayla. *Oh shit*, Kayla thought. It was Brenda Halt-storm, Jared's mother. Kayla prepared herself for a confronta-tion; the Indian women of Geshig were famously vicious when it came to their children and men.

But Brenda did not look angry. In fact, she looked sad, em-barrassed, and unquestionably drunk. Kayla softened her grip on Jared's shirt and placed it lightly over his shoulder.

"I'm sorry," Brenda said, trying to cover the slur. "He can get out of hand."

Kayla blinked and had no idea what to say to the drunken woman. It was noon on a Wednesday at a public park. Not un-common to see day drinkers around, but rarely were they moth-ers out with their children. Behind her, Hazel approached with her toddler close behind her skirt.

"Hello, Brenda," Hazel said in a calm, almost detached voice. "Looks like the boys got a little carried away."

"I'm sorry. I've told him he has to play nice."

Kayla glanced at Hazel for a moment, long enough to see there was no worry in her eyes. Pity, but no worry. She patted Jared's shoulder and urged him toward his mother. The boy stomped past her and went over to the far side of the park. He sat in the grass and began ripping up dandelions. Kayden and the other kids ran in the other direction.

"He's difficult," Brenda said, her tongue tripping over the word. "I don't know why but he'll be fine around other kids for like an hour and then just ..."

"Don't even worry about it," Kayla said. "Mine could use a whooping or two sometimes." She chuckled awkwardly, but still could not wrap her head around the woman's state.

To break the tension, Hazel picked up her son and held him out to Brenda. "Mine's not quite a troublemaker yet."

"Oh for cute! He looks just like you," Brenda said. She accepted the boy into her arms and rocked him. He didn't cry but the unfamiliar person seemed to scare him into a wide-eyed silence. "What's your name, little guy? How come I've never seen you around?" It only took the sound of her voice, despite the slur, to unfreeze his stare.

"This is Marion. I'm sorry you haven't met him yet. I don't really do much outside of work," Hazel said.

It was then Kayla remembered that Hazel was related to the Haltstorms, the bloodline her grandfather called the disgraces of Geshig. They were no worse than other troubled families, Kayla knew from her job at the Languille Lake Human Services Department. She handled lots of welfare cases, and enough with prosecutable fraud to know there were plenty of other families that could be described as disgraceful.

Still, sometimes they did live up to their reputation.

Hazel put her arm around Brenda and began to walk her away from the loose gravel of the park and toward another bench. Kayla had no idea how she could be so calm with her child being held by someone who had been drinking, but some other Lafourniers weren't beyond reservation gossip either. Not Hazel, but certainly her mother, Eunice, had—

No, Kayla thought. *That's Grandpa talking.*

She walked over to Kayden and pulled him away from the other children. They had already begun another game of football, the previous fight forgotten easily.

"You okay, honey?" She brushed the dirt and grass off his clothes and hair.

"Yeah. Jared's weak. I can take him."

"Stop it. You don't need to be taking anyone. You're lucky I don't take you home right now."

"He started it."

"He didn't. I saw what happened. You start playing nice."

"I will." He glanced at the group waiting for him. "With them."

"With everyone, or you'll never get to play ball again."

She sent him on his way and the game resumed. Near the edge of the park, Hazel watched Brenda and Jared leave, hopefully toward their home or somewhere safe.

On the grass, Kayden was tackled by another boy but this time they laughed.

The Junkman

BRENDA HALTSTORM HAD LITTLE trouble finding someone to watch her children when she needed a break. Being a mother of three was hard work, especially with the youngest barely out of diapers and the oldest with so much energy.

Jared had just turned ten, Natalie was six, and Tasha four. Each of their fathers had failed at the minimum job requirement: attendance. So, she raised them herself, with the occasional help from her many cousins and other family.

Today she brought them to the home of her cousin Bert, just a couple of short blocks from their town house by the railroad. The four walked into the yard and as soon as they saw him, Jared and Natalie yelled "Bert the junkman!"

He gave his usual nicotine-coated laugh and took them into his arms. His blue overalls had faded oil stains and his shirt was looking rather greasy and yellow instead of the original white, but the kids never minded how he looked. They loved everything about the place, from the rows of broken cars and appliances to the cheap swing set near the back door. It was always an adventure to them.

"I'll be back before dark," Brenda said. "Behave for your uncle!"

Bert brought the three children inside and the first thing he did was give them each a Tootsie Pop. Jared carefully inspected each one but couldn't find the Indian guy on the wrappers.

Unlike the outside of Bert's house, inside was neat and orderly. Jared sat down on the couch and the girls sat in front of the TV. Bert changed the channel from racing cars to a cartoon. But it was a girlie show with horses and rainbows, so neither Jared nor Natalie was interested. Tasha couldn't look away.

"Can we play outside?" Jared asked Bert.

"Only if you promise to stay away from the King," Bert said. "And don't leave the yard."

"Okay."

Jared grabbed Natalie's hand and led her outside. First they went to the swing set, but Jared hated having to always push his sister. She wouldn't listen to him when he tried to teach her how to swing herself so his arms got tired and it wasn't much fun for him.

He grabbed the rusty brown chains just above her fingers, stopped the swing, and whispered into her ear. "Let's play under the cars!"

She giggled but shook her head. "Mommy says we can't."

"You don't need to listen to her," Jared said. He gripped the chains harder. "She doesn't care what we do when she leaves."

He urged her off the swing and then ran for a blue-and-white truck that had concrete blocks instead of wheels. "Can't catch me!"

Her little footsteps followed but he was crawling underneath the truck and out from under on the other side before she reached it. Jared turned back before he crawled under the next car and saw she was still following.

They crawled under the cars, in and out and under, but never on top so the junkman wouldn't see them. Jared had to let her catch him sometimes otherwise she would cry and stop playing.

After a while, he grew bored and looked to the far corner of the yard. He felt her catch up to him under a big green van and grab his ankle. "Got you!"

"Let's go see the King," he whispered. He stared at the chain-link fence and smiled.

"No! Uncle said don't!"

"You don't have to listen to him either," Jared said. "Grown-ups don't know what they're talking about."

"I don't want to ..."

"I'll protect you." He looked around the yard and found a short and thin stick of metal. "He can't touch us."

Natalie hid behind him as they walked toward the fence. Inside was a big doghouse made of plywood with red paint and a bunch of old straw. On the roof of the house was a thick black rope, and at the end of the rope was the King.

His fur was dark gray like a storm cloud and his ears, once floppy, were cropped to look like little points. On his neck was a gold choke collar that sank into the gray folds of his skin. His eyes were droopy and bright pink.

At first the King didn't see them but when they got within a few feet he leaped to his feet and crashed into the edge of the fence, barking and snarling right into their faces.

Natalie screamed and ran back. Jared just laughed. He ran back and forth and the King followed him. His kennel was not large, but to Jared's short legs the distance he ran and taunted was miles. He began to run the metal tube against the fence and further annoy the dog.

His barks became louder, angrier. He wasn't just a dog. He was like a werewolf. The wolf wants to kill me! Jared thought.

In the corner of his eye he saw Bert come running around the rows of cars. In his hand was his belt, folded in half and hungry for skin. Jared ran farther to the corner of the yard, jumped onto a truck, and then over the fence.

Bert reached the truck and screamed through the chains. "You stay away too, you little shit!"

Jared ran toward the woods behind the train tracks. He hid behind a big oak tree and watched until he was certain the junkman wasn't following him. He walked farther back in the woods until he found a mossy stump, wet and rotted.

He hacked at the stump with the metal tube until it was nothing but squishy splinters, laughing, coughing, and then, finally, crying.

Ikwe (Woman)

KAYDEN FIRST LEARNED ABOUT papier-mâché in fourth grade, and soon began to waste his mother's frybread flour. He mixed it with water just like his teacher told him to, and it worked. Kayla walked into the basement and saw white-powdered footsteps on the concrete and prepared to yell.

"Play with me!" Kayden said.

On the table was what looked to be the lid of a shoebox with a paper pillar on each end. Strips of newspaper held the pillars to the lid with the flour paste. At the top of the pillars were loops made from red construction paper, like the paper he used for the Christmas calendar he made every year.

"What is it?" Kayla asked, less angry and more intrigued.

"It's a basketball court," Kayden said. "And these are my basketballs!" In the bottom half of the shoebox were several pale orange lumps with black dots in sinuous patterns. She could still smell the Sharpie in the air.

"What did you make these out of?"

"I found some cotton balls in the bathroom. Then I papiermâchéd them and colored them with this." Kayden held up an orange highlighter.

Kayla's anger was nullified by the swelling of pride and amusement. For the next half hour, she and her son threw crusted highlighter basketballs across the table. She could not make a single toss into the construction-paper hoop, but Kayden made almost every one. Or perhaps she only thought they were going through.

She had spent long hours watching Kayden throw his mini-basketball into the Fisher-Price hoop in the driveway. He had a great eye for accuracy. Already a basketball star, she thought, as her first papier-mâché ball landed her a point.

"You need to ask Mommy's permission next time, Kayden." Her attempt at scolding was as soft as the cotton balls he hadn't covered in flour. "You made a real mess down here." She brushed a strand of his hair away from his face. He gave her his big smile and made a promise that he would forget by the time he came up for dinner.

"I'll clean up my messes from now on."

When he sat at the kitchen table, his hair was full of flour and he wore a papier-mâché mask with pointy ears.

"Are you a puppy?" Kayla asked.

"No! I'm Anubis! I'm the Egyptian god of mummies!"

"I think you'd be cuter as a puppy."

"I am not cute, woman! I will harvest your soul!"

Kayla stared at her son in shock. Not because of the mortality threat—by now she was used to the weird things boys said—but because of the way he'd said *woman*.

It was a quick snap of the word, like it was one syllable. *Wum'n.*

She had heard it said many times growing up, her grandpa Vin always ordering around his wife, Georgina.

Make my dinner, *woman*! Hurry up and get ready, *woman*!

"Kayden *Vincent* Kelliher." She grabbed his mask from off his face and put it on the table. "You don't take that tone with me. You behave. Wolf masks aren't allowed at the dinner table."

"But he's not a wolf. He's a jackal."

"It doesn't matter. You learn some respect while we eat."

She decided against specifically telling him not to say the word *woman*, so he wouldn't think of it like a swear word. Maybe he was too young to know why she didn't want him talking like that. Maybe there was a different way to teach him.

When they were done eating, an idea came to her.

"Kayden, would you like to learn how to sing and dance, like at the powwow?"

He put on the jackal mask. "Kayden doesn't want to dance, woman! But Anubis does!"

"Okay. We're going to teach you how to dance."

In the basement, she made him clean every inch of flour without helping him.

SuperAmerica

WHEN JARED WAS TWELVE, most of Brenda's cousins could no longer stand to watch him. He was disrespectful, wild, and had no self-control. At first Brenda thought she could handle it but once while she was hungover Jared screamed in her face and she felt actual fear.

It was so revolting and hurtful to feel scared of her own child, but it instantly gave her the idea that she knew would fix him.

Every weekend Jared would stay with his grandmother Clara. She was a typical Indian grandmother, more tomahawk than battle-ax, and she didn't take anyone's shit, especially a grandson's. The only problem was that Clara was Jared's paternal grandmother and by default she hated Brenda.

Asking the woman for help was justification for her attitude. But oddly enough, it improved their relationship since Clara now knew she held the moral high ground.

So, every Friday, Brenda would now drive Jared fifteen minutes west of Geshig into Half Lake. Clara lived right behind a SuperAmerica gas station on the south end of town.

The first time she dropped him off, she did not even stop to see if Clara was home. Jared got out of the car, slammed the door hard as he could, and glared at the back of the house.

Clara walked out just as Brenda drove off. She was wearing pale pink shorts and a pink T-shirt with darker pink stripes. She was a tall, stout woman with a drawn face, like an English bulldog. She refused to accept her age by getting the old-lady haircut, so her salt-and-pepper strands fell just above her breasts.

"Get inside, boy. You have dishes to do."

Jared smiled and walked inside. He dropped his backpack of clothes in the entryway and refused to take off his shoes. At first he tried walking straight to the couch in the living room, but he felt her hand crush his shoulder and hold him back.

"I said dishes."

"I don't give a fuck what you said, bitch."

She whipped him around, slapped him on the cheek, and

grabbed his lower jaw. "I'm not your mom. You listen in this house. No *or else*. You just listen."

Jared took a swing at her. She caught him by the wrist, dragged him to the kitchen sink, and held him there until his face was burning and wet with tears.

The first weekend passed without further incident. Jared struggled with what he thought about Clara. Did he respect her or fear her? Was he angry and silently plotting revenge or was he learning to behave? The next weekend, he still had no answer, but he did not feel changed. He was just glad to not be home where the girls were always screaming and his mom was always drinking.

It was the third weekend when Jared saw Lonnie by random chance.

After asking politely for permission to walk to the gas station and buy some candy, Jared saw his older cousin pass behind the store.

"Hey, little man! What are you doing here?"

Lonnie was a cousin that Jared had always liked seeing at family gatherings, but rarely did he see him anywhere else. He looked the same as ever, with loose-fitting clothes and a black beanie.

"I'm living with my gramma now. It's bullshit but better than being with my bitch-ass mom."

Lonnie laughed. "Look at you, talking all grown-up. Pretty soon you'll start smoking and drinking."

"I smoke!" Jared insisted.

"No, you don't. What are you, like ten?"

"I'm twelve! Go buy me a pack of Camels and I'll prove it to you."

"Ha. You're funny, kid. I gotta go, but I'll see you around, kay?"

Lonnie left and Jared was tempted to follow, but instead he just bought his candy and went back to Clara's house.

On the fourth weekend, he found Lonnie behind the gas station again, this time with some friends. They were all Indians just like Lonnie, and they wore the same black sweaters and hats. Jared knew enough from the talk and assemblies at school to know what was going on.

"Let me join," he said, walking right into the crowd of much-older boys. "I wanna join." There was laughter all around. "Whatever. I don't need to. I'll kick all your asses." He had only heard rumors about how gangs initiated new members, and he wanted to impress Lonnie, so he took a chance.

There was more laughter and a few *oohs* around, but Lonnie now looked serious. "You may not like her, but I got mad respect for your ma, little man, and I can't do that to her ... But shit, if you want to, don't let me stop you."

The other boys looked at each other, then at Lonnie, and when he gave a nod of approval, they threw Jared down and began kicking him. Right away his breath was gone, his tears were flowing, and his body bruised. All but his face.

When he finally stopped crying and was focused, only Lonnie was there. He walked Jared to his apartment, just a few blocks away.

"You know those guys weren't actually fighting you." He brought him an ice pack and a cold can of beer. "They were taking it easy." Jared drank it down easily, just like when Brenda was passed out and the fridge was his to raid.

"I'm weak."

"Kids are weak. You're too young."

"Lots of kids my age are in gangs."

"How do you know?"

"They tell me about it."

Lonnie sat back on the couch and laughed. "Dude, they're fuckin' liars. People in gangs don't tell you they're in gangs." He started to drink a beer and made Jared drink another one down.

"Why are you in a gang?" Jared asked.

"Because of this." Lonnie pulled up his sleeve. There was a tattoo of a feather and an arrow crossing. "I'm an *ogichidaa*. A warrior."

"I can be too."

Lonnie leaned over to his glass table and put his face over a line of powder. "Oh yeah?" There was a loud snort. "You dropped like a bitch back there."

"Then teach me how to fight."

Another loud snort, and now Lonnie's shoulders were bobbing up and down. "Okay. But you'll have to go through another, heh, initiation."

Lonnie reached for his fly and unzipped.

21

FROM THE FIRST TIME Faron Mykleseth taught Kayden how to play basketball, no other cousin was close to being Kayden's favorite. He was close as a brother—closer, as was common for many reservation families.

"We'll start easy," Faron said. He launched the basketball from just underneath the hoop. It floated straight up from his hands and bounced off the rim softly to Kayden. "Go, little man!" Kayden caught the ball and began to dribble toward the three-point line. He had barely run five feet when Faron's hard hands snatched the ball right back. The eighteen-year-old Faron knocked twelve-year-old Kayden flat on his ass, and the boy strained to hold in angry tears.

"Why'd you do that?" he shouted.

"You turned your back, little dude. No one is gonna give you a break in a real game, so get up and don't let it happen again."

Faron knew that Kayden would not find the coaching he needed in Geshig's middle school team. The high school put on a good show every year, not always the best, but never bad, and he knew from experience that middle school sports were more about friendship, obedience, and after-school-special bullshit. No coach would ever dare to push Kayden's limits.

He would have coached him slower had he not already been enlisted. Marine Corps. Operation Iraqi Freedom. When Faron donned that uniform for the first time, he knew what it meant to be a warrior. He would make his whole family proud. His own veteran father, and the grandfather he and Kayden shared. Vincent Kelliher was the epitome of a warrior in both their eyes, and Faron would make him proud, live or die.

The funeral for the twenty-one-year-old Faron Mykelseth was held in the Geshig auditorium.

It was a community event, with coverage from all over the

state and every bleacher filled with mourning patriots. This was the price of freedom, said the reverend who officiated. This is God's will, no matter how painful or confusing it may seem.

Kayden Kelliher was listed as an honorary pallbearer. In private he told his mother he could not handle the task of escorting Faron's casket and burying him, so he walked behind the group as they brought it out of the gym and outside for one last salute.

All Kayden could do as the guns rang out in the parking lot was stare at the flag-covered coffin as the group waited behind the hearse. His eyes burned red as the stripes, and his tears were no longer being held back. They dropped from his eyes and slammed onto the ground like basketballs.

His grandfather was not crying. He held stone-faced as he aimed the rifle into the air and saluted his fallen kin. Kayden glared at his grandpa, his once-hero, and didn't know why he was so angry.

This was bittersweet. This was what it meant to be a warrior. A freedom fighter. An *ogichidaa*.

For the first time in his brief life, Kayden Kelliher did not wish to be an *ogichidaa*.

Indoodem (My Clan)

WHENEVER JARED RAN AWAY from home, he would walk toward St. Eric's Church on the east end of town. The Catholic presence in the town had always been small, and the dilapidated church had eventually been abandoned in favor of a smaller, inconspicuous building that most passersby mistook for a gas station.

Half a block behind the skeletal church, up a short driveway with tire marks bored into the dirt, and partially hidden by white lilac bushes was their real home.

It was not a nice home, barely better than the cracker-box housing of the north-side ghetto, but it was enough private space for the clan.

Lonnie hated the word *gang* ever since the first time Jared uttered it years ago. When he bought the house—the details of which he wouldn't reveal—he relocated all his operations back to Geshig and made his own rules. No one said the word *gang* around Lonnie, not his older brother, not Jared, not even his uncle Levi who was known as the strongest fighter on the reservation.

Jared joined the clan with a greenish-gray feather tattoo on his shoulder. No name or other marking, just a fine-lined plume and the knowledge of what it meant. They called themselves the Debwewin Ogichidaag. The True Warriors. They did not care about the white laws of the nation, and strived to live according to their own code. As much as a group of high schoolers could do.

Jared just got out of juvie for petty larceny when he heard about the fire.

The official report printed in the *Geshig Herald* listed the incident as accidental, resulting from faulty drug-cooking equipment. It was well-known among the clandestine users of Geshig that Lonnie Barclay wasn't just a dealer; he cooked meth himself. According to the fire marshal, the oven he was using to heat the chemicals caught fire, exploded, and the sole inhabitant was burned to death. Never stood a chance in the blaze.

Jared did not go to Lonnie's funeral because he couldn't afford a bus ticket to the distant reservation where his cousin was from. His grandmother would be no help, having decided she would never speak to him after his latest stay in lockup. And Brenda was probably whoring herself out for her next drink, he thought angrily, bitterly, as the tears fell onto the dark ash where Lonnie's house once stood.

But Jared knew the fire marshal was wrong. This was no accident. Lonnie wasn't stupid, and there was no doubt in Jared's mind that this couldn't have happened to him on his own.

Thanks to his grandmother's rants and ravings against every tribal politician she knew of, Jared knew where to follow the trail of corruption. The fire marshal was in the pocket of the Anders County sheriff, who was in the pocket of the reservation itself, which was run by the council. And the current tribal chair was one Lindale Kelliher, whose family was pushing as many drugs as they claimed to be fighting.

Jared went over the facts his grandmother told him until he concluded two things: This was arson. And the arsonist would pay.

Drum and Dance

ON HIS FIFTEENTH BIRTHDAY, Kayden brought a leather pouch full of pipe tobacco to his drum teacher.

"Will you find me a name?" he asked her in Ojibwe. Cecilia

made sure she did not cry at the request, accepted the *asemaa*, and later that night searched for Kayden's real name. When she found it, she planned a celebration dinner for the immediate Kelliher family, as was custom.

Kayla Kelliher had signed Kayden up for Drum and Dance the day after he called her *woman*, and every Wednesday night he learned from Cecilia Aysibohn what most Indian boys would learn from men. For that exact reason, it was a small class. No parents had said it out loud, but the attendance was down to less than a quarter of what it was the year before.

Cecilia Aysibohn's drumming caused controversy during the first powwow she attended, but it never stopped her from the beat. There was further controversy when she became the music instructor at Geshig High School.

Whoever heard of such a thing? A woman on the drum, pounding the taut, dried skin and wailing out the songs only men were meant to.

At least in Geshig there was controversy. Some reservations did not have the same sort of taboo, but to cover her ass, Cecilia asked permission from a medicine man to sing. Or so she claimed. Whenever she was asked who gave her the blessing to take a man's seat at the drum, she gave a different name. There was no database of accredited elders or spiritual leaders in North America. If the name and the story sounded correct, who was to stop Cecilia Aysibohn from singing or teaching?

But Kayden didn't care about who was teaching once he saw the *dewe'igan*. He had never drummed before but at first sight of the big circle of splotched brown hide, he ran to a seat, picked up a drum beater, and sang.

His first attempt at sound was a series of loud, monotone *yahs* that had Cecilia holding back her laughter. It seemed as if his voice was not the type for powwow singing, but she would not discourage him.

In time, Kayden found his voice but his dancing was specialized. He couldn't move to any beat with his legs, clumsy and wild as a spider, but on the basketball court he was as graceful as a shawl dancer. The town watched Kayden glow on the court, and Cecilia saw it in a dream.

"I dreamed the name Waasegiizhig. Glowing Sky," she announced at his dinner.

"Oh." Kayden laughed uncomfortably. "I lost ten bucks. I bet my mom it would be the Wolfman."

Though he was good at pretending, she noticed the slight fall of his smile when she said it out loud the first time. Disappointment. He was a young man, after all, and he probably wanted a name that made him sound tough. But her dream did not lie. She took him aside and told him what was rightfully only meant for his ears.

"I saw this town in my dream. I saw a great curtain of fog roll over, but it was black like smoke. But wherever you walked, the smoky fog went away. You're the future, Kayden, the light of the town. Geshig. Waase*giizhig*…"

The big points of his teeth finally showed in his smile, and he hugged her. "*Miigwech, gikinoo'amaagewikwe.*"

Cecilia was so overwhelmed with pride and gratitude, so focused on watching the light amid that fog, that she didn't think it strange when Kayden did not leave the party with his mother.

Instead, Kayden left with his cousin Dominic, who he told to meet him at the door near the end of the party.

Far out of town, away from the town's silly dancing and basketball, Kayden, Dominic, and a handful of other boys began to crack open bottles of malt liquor around a campfire. Though he was not supposed to reveal it just yet, the others coaxed and hazed him into telling them his new name.

"Ay! Waase!"

"Waasay!"

They raised their bottles to the name and saluted the gang.

"Indian Bloodz for life."

The light of Geshig clinked his bottle and concurred. "NDN Bloodz for life."

Medicine Wheel

THE FIRST STAB WAS the only one he felt and it was the only one needed for him to realize life was now minutes, if even. Kayden's life did not flash before his eyes; there were not enough memories for that. Instead, he had two thoughts, one for the future and one for the past.

His daughter or son, whatever it may be, he hoped they would be loved, be happy, and never experience this kind of pain. He would never hold a baby in his arms, something he had only done once before as a toddler. So, he thought of that and imagined instead it was his own.

Kayden prayed as hard as he could for the child in his arms, and when he was done he saw the red glow of the past. The bright glass beads on a bandolier bag, a medicine wheel. The color of *zhaawanong*, the south. The color of a red-hot sun that was setting and leaving behind nothing but dirt on a darkling hill. Instead of flat on the ground, Kayden felt his body was now leaning against that hill and above him, the face of the girl he loved. She refused to climb the rest of the way without him but eventually was urged onward by small, shadowy hands on her stomach and as she reached the summit she did not look back.

The beads on the medicine wheel shattered, and Kayden felt himself drift into the air from the second hill of summer to deep black winter. He could see nothing but *ishpiming.* Up above. Slowly, points of light appeared. Not stars but not unlike stars. It was as if he was under a black sheet tattered with small holes, and through each shone the most beautiful light.

He felt his body fade away as he reached up to touch the sky.

Five

What Mothers Do

WHEN I WAKE UP, Shannon's body and arms are wrapped around me from behind and I'm sweating from the heat of his body. My head hurts and my throat is dry. Too much whiskey and weed. But I feel his chest moving and his breath on the back of my slick neck, and smile.

"You okay to talk yet?" I ask.

"Mmm, can't we just enjoy this?" He squeezes me tighter.

"I guess, but you're the one that wanted to come over."

"And I can still change my mind."

"Okay. But can we talk about anything?"

"Like what?"

"I don't know. Tell me about your job."

"It's a resort. There's a lake and there's woods. Not much to say ..." Goose bumps rush down my neck and I try to shake away from his wet grip. "Well, actually, we think there's been a wolf out there."

"Why?"

We peel our bodies away from each other. "We're finding a lot of dead animals around."

I watch Shannon get dressed. He wears tight gray boxer briefs with a shiny waistband and designer label. When we first met he only wore plain boxers with dull checkered designs but as the summer went on his attire became conspicuously smaller and more colorful. His overall hygiene and look improved too. Part of me does miss the smell of the lake and sweat that used to cling to him.

"What do you do with the remains?"

"I just find a spot in the woods and bury them."

"Has anyone seen the wolf?"

"There's been a few reports but it's always on the move. Did you see it?"

"A wolf? No." Not a lie. When he is fully dressed, he sits back on the bed. Usually he makes his getaway a lot quicker. His fingers are tapping on the mattress and his feet are tapping on the floor. He sighs. "I don't know what to say."

I lean over and run my fingers over his hand. "You could say why you keep coming over. You could say what you actually want."

"No answer for that either."

"Wife? Kids? Live in Geshig forever?"

"No, fuck no, and yes."

"What about . . ." I stop myself before I blurt out the word *husband*. "A boyfriend."

"That won't work."

"Is that an assumption or experience?"

"It's my family. Some things are better left unsaid."

I don't know much about the Harstads but it's not too far-fetched to imagine them as that kind of family, even on a reservation. Could be Christian, could be secular. If he thinks it's better to stay closeted to them, he probably knows their initial reaction wouldn't be good.

"Do you have anything to eat?" he asks.

"Haven't shopped lately. Just go through the kitchen and try whatever looks edible."

I drag myself out of bed and put on clothes while he rifles through the cupboards. I let Basil out the front door and then pick up my phone from the couch cushions where I left it last night. My mother has replied five times to my text, called twice, and has left one voice mail. Each message progressively gets more worried in that motherly kind of way that is sweet and overbearing. I call her right away without checking the voice mail.

She answers on the second ring.

"Hey, Mom. I'm doing fine."

"You need to start answering your phone more, brat."

Shannon peeks his head around the corner and watches me talk. "Sorry. I meant to reply last night but I was . . ." Shannon smiles. "Walking my dog."

"You haven't killed him yet?"

"No. He's doing fine."

"Anni says he'll take it off your hands anytime you want if you can't handle it."

"Stop trying to take my dog away."

"I'm just saying. So why did you ask to come down here? Is there something wrong?"

"No. Just wanted to see you. And Anni, I guess."

"Honestly, Marion, I don't know how a child of mine could be such a bad liar." I hear the loud, gruff laugh of my stepfather, Aanakwad, in the background. "Just head down when you're free and we'll talk."

"Okay. Love you."

"Love you too, kiddo."

When I hang up Shannon laughs. "You sounded like a kid just now."

"Shut up."

"I'm the same way when my dad calls me. Sometimes he needs help with yard work but it sounds like he's telling me rather than asking me."

In the kitchen, Shannon has made two sandwiches with peppered turkey. He has already bit into his. "What the hell kind of bread is this? It tastes like black licorice."

"Licorice? What? It's pumpernickel. It doesn't taste like licorice."

"Yes it does."

I take a bite of mine just to see if this loaf was made differently. I buy it from a small bakery downtown. "It's a sweet bread, but I don't know where you're getting the licorice taste. Can you finish it?"

"Yeah, it's fine. Just weird. We only get white bread, so I'm used to that."

"Yuck. This is way better."

In between bites, we sit in an awkward silence and give each other the occasional glance. It always slips my mind until moments like this that beyond the sex, we don't have much in common and even less to talk about. Probably the second most awkward breakfast I've had since moving back to Half Lake.

"Do you have cable? Wanna watch the game?"

"Sure." I have no idea what game he means. I assume football since it's that time of year, but it could be something else for all I know.

In the living room he grabs the remote, falls back on the couch, and flips through the channels. I let Basil back inside and he begins to pad around the house restlessly. At first I sit on the farther end of the couch, but Shannon motions for me to scoot closer. He pulls me over him so that the front of my body is on his and my head is between his chest and his arm.

"I have no idea what's going on," I tell him as the men on the screen pile on each other.

"Do you want me to explain?"

"You can." I bring my arm over his body and pull closer. "But I probably won't listen."

During the entire game the only thing I can pay attention to is the sound of his breathing.

━━━━

"I'LL SEE YOU IN a few days, boy." The rank smell of dog breath fills my nose as Basil licks my face. "Be good for Shannon ... Or shit on his floor."

"If he does, I'm putting it in your mailbox," Shannon says from the truck. I pet Basil one last time and shut the passenger door. It's one in the afternoon and cloudy, but still too bright to expect a nice goodbye from Shannon. He offers only a slight nod and then pulls away.

Less than twenty minutes later, I'm in my car and on the way to my mother's house. She lives two hours south of Half Lake. I would have brought Basil with me but I know the moment we get there we would be subject to a close inspection by Hazel and Anni. They'd question everything, how he's eating, if he's happy, his fur quality. Anything they can to make me look like a bad pet owner. Anni has been a dog trainer for years, so his way is the best way. As for Hazel, it's just her job to second-guess me.

It's been that way since the first dog we got, when I was old enough to actually take care of it. It was another mutt, a slim-faced and fluffy-furred yellow collie mix she got from one of her co-workers. It was sleeping on my pillow as a surprise when I got home. The real surprise was the wet stain that left me without proper head support for the night, but the pup was too adorable to be mad at.

My first name for her was Cassiopeia.

"That's too long for a dog's name, kiddo," my mother said.

"Fine. How about Eurydice?"

"That's only one syllable shorter."

"Persephone?"

"Why are you choosing these awful names?"

"They're not awful. They're Greek names. Goddesses." I held the dog up to my mother's face. "She's too pretty for a normal name."

"Your last dog name was better."

"Doggy? I was like nine."

"Yeah and it was cute. Simple. How about just Cassie?"

"You call her that. I'll call her Cassiopeia."

Just like with Basil, I spent most of my summer with Cassiopeia. She was much harder to train and wouldn't learn anything unless I tempted her with chunks of hot dog. I had barely taught her anything, just sitting and laying, by the time she left the yard and never came back. Even though I was in school when it happened, my mother seemed to think I had done something wrong. One of the many incidents that convinced her that I'm irresponsible.

When crossing into the reservation where my mother lives, and any reservation really, there is an interesting transformation. The land becomes a mix of feral beauty and man-made blight. On one side of the highway you can see nature at its finest and on the other, humans at their worst. Anni told me once that the colors of autumn were like paintbrush strokes and every year they convince him a little more that the Creator is real. The colors make up for the yards filled with broken-down cars, heaps of garbage, boarded-up windows, burned trailers, and basketball hoops held steady by cinder blocks.

I was fortunate enough to not live in those kinds of conditions growing up. My mother had inherited her mother's property on the south side of Lake Anders and all our neighbors were rich white snowbirds. Because her mother's side of the family had grown up in typical reservation fashion, my mother was obsessed with keeping a nice yard and house. I'm not sure if it was to impress white people or gloat to the family, but it gained her a bit of resentment from both.

It's early evening when I arrive at her house. A horde of five dogs run out from underneath a tall porch and surround my car. I step out to a chorus of barks that quiet as soon as Anni and my mother step outside.

The house is filled with the smell of Anni trying too hard to be Native. His meal consists of wild rice with blueberries, smoked venison, and frybread. Harvested the wild rice and blueberries himself and the deer meat is from the previous year's hunting season. Only the frybread's ingredients are store-bought. And the most amazing part to me is that my mother is not ashamed of the meal.

"We're not a frybread family," she would tell me growing up. When we would go to family gatherings, funerals, even school functions, she preferred that I did not eat it. To many, Indian and non-Indian, frybread is an endearing aspect of our culture. Indian tacos, frybread burgers, all those kinds of novelty foods found at powwows. She hated them.

"How did you get her to agree to this?" I ask Anni.

"I use olive oil. Makes it a little less bad."

I take a bite of the squishy bread and the taste is definitely not "less bad." It's rather bitter from a mix of the whole wheat, olive oil, and chia seeds. But if my mother approves of it, I would be rude not to finish.

"How is Basil?" she asks.

"He's great. No problems at all."

"Last time you called he was chewing shoes."

"Don't worry. I took out his teeth. He uses dentures now."

My mother's eyes widened. I forgot that Anni uses dentures. Luckily, he laughs about it. She shakes her head and a small smile forms. "So, if it's not your dog, what is it?"

"What do you mean?"

"You wanted to talk about something."

"I did. But now I don't."

"Is it a guy?"

I take big bite of the wild rice and glance at Anni. He doesn't have a typical Indian look. His hair is short and silver, and his skin is light. I've heard it said that this reservation has a lot more light-skinned members than most because of a lot of intermarriage during the relocation period, and if there is any truth to it, Anni is proof. Despite that, he's about as close to a traditionalist as I've met before, which is why I was surprised when she first started dating him a few years ago. I'm not close to him but I have no qualms about talking about men in front of him.

"Two boys, actually."

She sighs. "Marion …"

"Not what you think. So, I've been sort of seeing this guy …" I hesitate, not sure if I want to say his name. "Shannon."

"Shannon Harstad?"

Her remembering him makes me cringe. He would not be happy if he knew. "Uh, yeah. We've been hanging out on and off all summer but he won't—he's not, like, out to anyone."

"Why not?"

I shrug. "He never really says why. Family, job, who knows."

"And the other guy?"

Black marble glitters behind my eyes. "It's his roommate." I haven't said it out loud yet. "I think he's like, abusing him."

I explain to her the details, best as I remember them. Almost everything he has told me except for some of the anatomical specifics. "So, I don't really know what to do because Shannon won't talk about it. But he shouldn't be living there, should he?"

Before my mother can respond, Anni speaks up. "Marion, have you considered just staying out of the situation?"

"I—no. What good would that do?"

"Well, is there any good *you* should be worried about? It doesn't sound like Shannon thinks it's any of your business."

I pause and stare at my stepfather. "He all but admitted he was raped. By his roommate. Does it matter if that's not my business?"

"They're both grown men. They can work it out themselves." Anni continues eating as if what he said is completely fine.

"I think I agree, Marion," Hazel says. "About you not getting involved, I mean. These two sound dangerous."

I shake my head. "Forget it. Probably doesn't matter."

The conversation settles back to small talk about the dogs, Hazel's job, my job, Anni's latest project, things I don't mind changing the subject to. When the plates are cleared, Anni gets the dogs ready for their nightly walk.

"You two wanna join?"

"No thank you, dear. We're gonna catch up a little more," Hazel says.

"I understand." Anni nods and leaves us alone.

═══════

MY MOTHER TRIED TO hide her frequent pot smoking from me until I was sixteen. One day I had planned to stay at Amos's house for the night but that was around the time he and I had started drifting apart. I think I remember sitting in his basement, watching a movie, and having nothing to say to each other. He drove me home and made some half-hearted plans for a night that never happened.

When I walked onto the backyard patio overlooking the

silvery-black stain of Lake Anders, she was blazed out of her mind and still rolling another joint.

Her voice was slow and monotone and she barely looked at me as she said, "You can try some if you want. I won't get mad at you."

I hesitated for maybe ten long seconds in shock. It was not that I had never seen her high before. It was that after years of pretending she was the perfect white soccer mom, at least as close as an Indian woman could get, she asked me to join instead of trying to shelter me.

"Sure."

So, we smoked. First, I felt it in my chest. Not the smoke—I was used to tobacco smoke after a few drum groups and ceremonies during my "connect with my ancestors" phase—but the high. Something weird and shaky like my lungs being tickled from the inside. Then my mouth went dry and I couldn't concentrate. I couldn't even form a full sentence. "How do you like it?" my mother asked. I fell silent and just stared out at the dark water until out of nowhere with no sort of buildup she said, "It's okay if you're gay, Marion. You can tell me."

Maybe because I had found out what she thought was her secret, she thought it was okay to bring up what I thought was mine. But she'd always known.

I didn't say anything. Even through the new sensation swirling through me, I felt my body start to shake. But the sight of the lake and the trees was calming and I felt my head nod up and down, slow as a rusty seesaw.

Since then, I've known that if I want her to talk about something serious, it's easiest if we're both high. She only smokes when Anni isn't around. It's not a secret, just a courtesy to him.

I don't smoke as much as she does, so I still have trouble speaking sometimes. "Mom, do you, uh. Um. Remember—much about Kayden Kelliher?"

She takes a big bite of the weird, hipster-ish frybread, now cold and soggy like a half-eaten placenta. "He's dead."

"Well, yeah. But do you remember stuff about him?"

"Does it matter? It's all just memories."

I stare at her as she focuses on the greasy flap of bread. "You said you watched him when he was little. I thought you might know if he ever had a dog. Like a pitbull or something."

She shrugs. "I don't know. It was years ago."

"I guess. But are you sure you don't remember?" The question leaves my lips without thought.

"I try not to. Is that bad? Does that make me a bad mother? First Jace, then Kayden."

I have no answer for her.

Our family cemetery is filled with gravestones named Lafournier, Bullhead, Bellerose, and Haltstorm. My great-grandfather Tomas Haltstorm was orphaned after a fire and adopted by a French-Ojibwe man, Baptiste Lafournier. When Tomas grew up, he married a forest woman named Bullhead who refused to take his last name or rename her children from a previous marriage, but Tomas's children by her took his.

My mother says Tomas was asked if he'd like to keep his birth name and declined. I'm glad he did, not only because the Haltstorm name is rather disliked on our rez but because it's actually incorrect. Hallström means something like "rock stream" in Swedish but somewhere along the family tree the name was mistranslated into Haltstorm.

There is no name on the grave for Hazel's first son. He was stillborn at thirty-one weeks, and buried with a blank wooden cross. She did have a name picked out for him, Jace Hiram Lafournier. Just like her mother, she had no intention of giving her children their father's last name. I don't really know why.

On the rare occasions when her first child comes up, she always refers to him as "your brother." I don't have the heart to tell her that I've always hated this. It's uncomfortable, to say the least. I can't feel a familial connection to the non-memory of a stillborn child.

Though she was not shy about mentioning her first son, she did not tell me about how, to prepare for motherhood, she babysat her best friend Kayla's son, Kayden. She did not tell me how many months she spent with the happy and energetic boy who never sat still unless it was dinnertime. She never told me how much he meant to her until after he was gone.

After a few minutes pass in smoky silence, we walk outside. One of the dogs has been left behind, a lazy Saint Bernard named Kuba. Last time I was here, back in July, he was completely shaved after an altercation with a thistle bush, but he has regained his white-and-ginger fluff.

She doesn't look at me when she speaks, only at Kuba. "I haven't thought about him in years."

"Sorry. I should've asked you in a better way."

"Is there such thing when it comes to dead kids?"

"Maybe."

"Do you remember when I would bring you over to Kayla's

house? Me and her would play cribbage and you wouldn't leave the kitchen to play with the other kids in the house."

"I don't, really. I think I remember the table. And cigarette smoke."

"After a while I just kind of stopped talking to her ... It didn't seem fair. That before, we were mothers and that's what we would do. Be mothers together and talk about our kids, but then one day, she wasn't anymore." She stops petting Kuba and then looks at me with a sad smile. "Kayden did not have a dog. When I was pregnant with you, I wanted to get a puppy to help me prepare. Kayla told me Kayden was allergic, so I couldn't bring one to their house. Why did you wanna know?"

"Just wondering."

"Bad liar. What's going on?"

I choose my words carefully so I don't raise any serious alarms. "A dog spirit led me to Kayden's grave and I don't know why." Being high helps too.

Before the merry-go-round, I didn't give a lot of thought to these things. Hazel was always closer to our culture than me, smudging our house with sage every so often and believing in certain signs. An eagle flying above our house or during a powwow. House noises at night meaning ghosts or spirit orbs. And something about a jawbone. But hers was only a basic belief, more going through the motions than truly valuing it all.

"I don't really know what to tell you other than it was probably stupid to chase a spirit."

"Gee, thanks. You're a great medicine woman."

I thought she would laugh, but her eyes are glazed over and shining. "I used to think it was Bullhead's curse. You remember?"

I nod. Hazel's grandmother Bullhead was a mystery among the families she begat. Only Tomas knew where she came from, saying he found her "in a sacred grove." She had two children; no one knew who the father was, but there was one nasty rumor that few would mention.

"The jawbone, right?"

"Yeah. My aunts, they liked to talk about it more than your grandmother did. No matter who I talked to, it never really changed."

The story is about some unknown white man who kidnapped her and forced her into marriage. After the birth of the second baby, she slit his throat, cut out his jawbone, and left. When Tomas Lafournier found her later and brought her back to Geshig, she kept the jawbone and fed it small scraps of food every day like a spirit dish, but then after she died no one knew where it ended up.

"Your grandmother used to say that all the Lafournier and Bullhead women were cursed to kill their men. But after Kayden died, I couldn't help but think maybe that was it. Maybe just by being around him, our bad medicine leaked to him." She dabs a few small tears from her eyes. "Silly. Silly Hazel, silly Eunice ..."

Kuba begins to whine and lets out a pitiful bark before crawling underneath Hazel's seat. Her eyes grow stiff and she stares across the yard.

"Marion. Is that the dog?"

I roll my eyes and sigh. "Seriously?" But sure enough, when I turn and look across the yard, there it is. Standing at the edge of the woods and staring at me.

No. His gaze is for my mother. "I don't think that's a dog,

Marion." Her voice is airy and slow, more than usual even for being high. "It's a wolf."

Without another word, Hazel stands up, walks to her car, and drives away. The Revenant at the edge of the yard watches her until the lights disappear, and then turns back to me.

In the distance, half a dozen barks crack across the night and the Revenant runs away. When Anni and his pack arrive back at the porch, Kuba finally comes out from under the seat.

———

"DID THIS DOG MAKE contact with you at all?"

"Yes. It looked really feral at the graveyard, so I approached it slowly with my hand out like this. It let me pet it and then it ran away without a trace." There is enough truth to that statement. I did play with the dog for a while after it came back to life, so if coming in contact with it means something I doubt the timing of it matters much.

Anni and I are sitting in the kitchen, waiting for a pot to boil. He remained calm when I told him what happened to Hazel, and then, because he demanded to know everything, I told him the full story of the dog.

"Did you know that *manidoo* means mystery?" he says. "Spirits are that, son. Impossible to understand. You can't know for sure if this *manidoo* means you harm or is evil."

"Wouldn't it have killed me by now if it was evil?"

"Part of the mystery. What if it's planning something, needs you alive for now?"

"Then I guess I can't do much about it."

"Wrong." From a glass container on the table, he grabs a tree branch with needles that look like vibrant green chains.

I shrug. "Okay, sure. What kind of magic do you have for me?"

When the tea is done steeping, Anni pours it into a wooden mug and hands it to me. "Back when I was on meth," he begins, "my family decided for me that I was going to quit. They kept me in their basement and made sure I didn't get any more in my system. I'm lucky the meth only got my teeth and not the rest of me. To this day, I swear I would have died of withdrawals if it wasn't for my uncle's cedar tea. It's a cleanser."

I take a drink. It tastes like I've licked a pine-needle air freshener.

"She still hasn't answered." Anni stares at his phone screen like it is an enemy. "I mean, no offense, kiddo, but since you brought that thing here do you think you might know where your mother went?"

Kiddo.

Ever since Hazel first met Anni, he has called me son or bud or sometimes *ingozis*. But only Hazel can call me kiddo.

"No idea. Maybe back to Geshig? Back to Lake Anders?"

"My first thought too, but she hated that cabin."

"I know."

"I'm not worried about her," he says. "I just can't really sleep without her. Around three a.m. I probably will worry."

"So, what's this supposed to cleanse me of? Undead-dog rabies?"

"I don't know, but if there was anything bad from the dog this'll take care of it."

"Like, lingering bad-spirit pollen?"

"You and your jokes."

"I'm sorry. I'm just not into all this ... tradition."

"Oh, I can tell you stories about people who weren't lucky enough to know the old ways. Men killed by *wiindigoog*. Children kidnapped by the *memegwesiiwag*. Mothers who touched dead bodies and then cursed their babies."

I almost choke on the tea. "Wait, what? What about dead bodies?"

"If you touch a dead body, you shouldn't touch a child before washing your hands in cedar tea. Bad things can happen. The person's spirit might try to take the baby with them. I've seen it. Nothing but a black stain on the bedsheets is left."

Another memory comes back, not my own, but something my mother told me about.

Kayden was buried in a blue-and-white star quilt, one he'd had since birth, and his funeral was held at the Gizhay Manido Chapel, with a reverend who spoke to Jesus and an elder who prayed in Ojibwe to the Great Spirit. Despite no previous tension between the families, no one related to the Haltstorms showed up, they only sent flowers and donations.

Except for Hazel, the woman who used to babysit young Kayden in preparation for the child she was expecting. As a Lafournier who didn't really associate with the Haltstorms, she was welcome. She didn't make me go with her, but she told me all about it.

At the open casket, she kissed Kayden on the forehead and put a beaded medallion on his chest. A gift for his journey. When she came home, she held me in her arms and cried, saying she never wanted me to leave the house again. Never leave Geshig. In my mind, I asked, *Why not leave here if this is the town that killed Kayden?* Aloud I just said okay, over and over. I would never leave her.

She held me for a while longer, and then, just as she had with Kayden, kissed me on the forehead.

I look at my reflection in the black tea. "Anni, when you say 'child,' just how old do you mean?"

Six

Just for Today

IT STARTED ON THE morning of the last day of the Geshig
Labor Day Powwow.

Somehow, Brenda's current work shift had turned her into a
morning person. She never got home before midnight and rarely
fell asleep before one a.m., but she always woke up at nine a.m.
sharp. Perhaps only by coincidence it was the same time the Red
Pine Diner opened its doors, though it didn't start serving alco-
hol until eleven.

Brenda knew this as she dismounted her van and walked into
the diner, ordering a Denver omelet, hash browns, and black coffee. She figured she would have plenty of time to eat and be on
her way before the temptation of the taps opened.

And she did. Her plate was finished by ten o'clock and she
spent the next half hour reading the previous day's *Geshig Herald*.
Absolutely nothing new was happening in town. It was just as
cyclic and unchanging as usual, but after many years of not being able to handle the news, she now read it as often as she could.

Right as she finished the crimes report, a woman sat across from her.

"Who's this dirty ol' bitch?" she said.

Brenda looked up and saw her cousin Henrietta for the first time in three months. She was wearing a dark blue flannel and jeans, and her once ink-black hair was peppered with silver at the roots. Brenda's own hair had begun to go this way long ago— either stress or just being forty-seven—but a frequent dyeing routine kept that hidden.

"The bitch that always kicked your ass growing up," Brenda replied. "How you been?"

"Same as ever. Still at the tables. You still scrubbing toilets?"

Brenda had been working as a housekeeper in the hotel and casino just outside of town. For three years she had managed to keep the job, longer than any of her other jobs at the casino, and she had no plans to break that streak. "Every day. And they're finally letting us keep the tips guests leave behind."

"What's that, like a buck and their leftover pizza?"

"On a good day."

"I keep telling you to deal. Our tips are like a thousand a night at Magic."

"Nah, I'm fine where I'm at."

It was the first time in many years that Brenda could say that sort of thing and mean it. She had a steady job, a cozy house, and her children were not constantly hitting her up for money any-more. Life was comfortable, and Brenda had no desire to change that.

Henrietta led a different kind of life. For the next half hour, she filled Brenda in on the turbulence of the past few months.

She and the two children she had custody of had been kicked out of her mother's house, and the father of her other two children had rescinded her visitation rights. Her children had stolen her wallet and spent the remainder of her paycheck on cigarettes and beer, bought by an older cousin. She spent one night in the drunk tank and barely avoided another by sweet-talking the reservation cop with the as-of-yet unfulfilled promise of a wild night.

Brenda watched her cousin thoughtfully while she prattled, but her ears were barely attentive. It was nothing out of the ordinary for most of her family members, and probably better since Henrietta managed to stay employed through the ordeal. She even had some cash on hand, which she used to buy two bottles of beer.

"Oh no, that's fine," Brenda said as the waitress left their table behind. "I'm okay with water."

"C'mon, you can have just one."

"It's not even noon."

"We're old bitches now. We don't need to pretend we care about five o'clock."

Brenda did not enjoy being called an old bitch, especially by a cousin older than her. Henrietta laughed and prodded more and more. Brought up this party and that one and how the two used to be.

"Remember when we stole a watermelon from Nelson's? Brought it all the way across town and smashed it on the train tracks."

"Must have been you. I don't steal shit."

"You hid it in your shirt!"

Brenda rolled her eyes, tapped her fingers, and sighed. What was there to be nostalgic about if she could hardly remember those days? Those blackout nights. Sticky hangover mornings. The only clear memories were how sick she could make herself, yet still get up and start over.

"Just for old times, since we're old-timers now," Henrietta pleaded one last time.

When the waitress came back with two frosty green bottles, Brenda followed in the footsteps of the many old barflies she had known since childhood and had a drink before noon. She thought about her book of meditations from AA class. All those inspirational quotes that started with *Just for today. Does that work both ways? Just for today I can drink.*

She had barely had a sip when the doors to the diner opened and a family walked inside. Gerly Pokegama, her daughter, Maya Kelliher, and Maya's grandmother Kayla, all three beautiful and fine-skinned. The Kellihers married and bred young. Maya's father, Kayden, even died young thanks to her son, Jared, a thought that made her take another drink. And another until her one drink became two, and Brenda's old dance began.

The familiars came back, the lightness on her skin like small drafts in winter, the warmth that began in her shoulders and spread in every direction, and finally the laughs. She and Henrietta were soon cackling at everything they said to each other. But her self-consciousness did not disappear with her sobriety. She wasn't even sure if they saw her, but she wanted to leave the sight of the Kellihers quickly.

Fifteen minutes and one phone call later, tabs paid, and a scatter of green bottles on the plastic cloth covering the picnic table, Brenda and Henrietta stepped into a reservation transport van. The bingo shuttle. The last vehicle Indians from Geshig would see before the hearse.

Brenda scrambled into the back seat and tried to sit upright but on the first turn, her head became heavy as a ball of dough. She flopped onto the seat and closed her eyes. She laughed silently to herself and thought about her children.

All three, Jared, Natalie, and Tasha, were born to be dancers. The potential in them had shone brightly all through their youth and then slowly tapered away with the onset of puberty. Natalie and Tasha both stopped dancing around their teen years, Jared before ten.

As soon as she began to walk, Natalie did not like to stop moving. Her movements were fast and clumsy, and she would stomp around the house like a yearling in summer. Tasha was a late bloomer when it came to just about everything, and walking took her a lot longer than her older sister. But such patience and shyness gave her an easier, gentler gait.

When the music played, their polarities switched. Natalie's feet were precise with the beat, and her posture was perfect for the jingle dress. She danced with pride holding up her shoulders and even after the last beat she did not break her statuesque composure. As soon as she was off the circle, she was back to her wild, clumsy self.

Tasha was not a wild child. She did not like to roughhouse with her sister, and she would not set foot near her cousins who were rougher than Natalie ever was. Typical for the youngest child, Brenda's mother and aunt said. The girl was a gentle shadow behind her mother, until the day in Headstart when she was given an electric-pink shawl with blue butterflies.

Tasha flapped the shawl above her head like a startled chicken and screamed as she twirled in circles on the grass. It was as if the tiny gossamer sheet had freed her. She had no rhyme or reason to her movements and rarely stopped at the end of the song. But that's okay, Brenda thought, when she saw her youngest child at her first powwow. The Tiny Tot dance was not a place for precision or judgment. It was pure innocence, and seeing her shadow come to life was one of the proudest moments in her life.

Now the bingo shuttle came to a sudden stop and Brenda rolled right off the seat and onto the mossy gray floor dappled with cigarette burns.

"You okay, ho?" Henrietta's face popped over the seat and stared at the drunken mess she had created.

"I'm fine!" Brenda struggled to pull herself out of the tight space, finally managing to use a broken seat-belt strap as leverage. "I wanna dance!"

"Ain't that kind of party, *niij*. Act sober or we'll get kicked out." Henrietta opened the van doors and smacked Brenda right on the ass as she jumped out onto the powwow grounds.

The pungency of fried food, tobacco, and campfires hit her. Even without seeing the whirlpool of Indians walking around the outer circle, she could tell it was a powwow with just a whiff. It used to remind her of home. Not her cozy shack, but that opaque sense of love and contentedness that she felt for brief moments when her children were young.

"Wanna get a hot dog?" Henrietta said. "I know you love a mouth full of wiener."

Brenda draped her arm over her cousin's shoulder and began to lead her toward one of the many concession stands at the edge of the circle. "We better get a few so you can sit on one in the bleachers."

The two women laughed their way through the gate and into the circle. The events were usually heavily guarded to prevent this very situation, and this holiday weekend was no different, but being that Grand Entry had just started the guards were less inclined to make a scene or peel their eyes away from the high school girls.

Brenda and Henrietta stopped a few yards away from the inner circle, just behind the opening between two bleachers. For just a few seconds, Brenda could see the eagle staff and American flag in the center. The old men of the honor guard were dancing in place, feet stomping to the beat, and the next group of dancers were mixing in. The regalia shimmered with every color under the sun.

The moment was short lived as Henrietta took control of their conjoined adventure and led her farther around the circle. They passed three frybread stands before Henrietta decided on a rusty blue-and-white stand called Paula's Perfect Breadstand, written in thick black Sharpie.

Hearing the crackle of the fryers and smelling the thick scent of flour suddenly made Brenda lose her appetite. Any dish that was served with the crustified paste that only rarely resembled real bread would have made her sick. Henrietta ordered an Indian taco loaded with every fixing they had, lettuce, jalapeños, diced tomatoes from a can, olives, sour cream, and Sam's Club mild taco sauce.

Brenda ordered a bowl of hominy soup and hoped she could keep it down while Henrietta ate her own sloppy pile of grease.

She stared at her first spoonful and wondered if it was worse than a taco. The chunk of ham was girthy and pink, with a strip of blackened skin on the end and a gelatinous worm of fat between skin and meat. The white puffs of hominy looked like punched-out toddler's teeth.

The soup stayed down and Henrietta ate every part of the taco including the sauce on the bottom of the Styrofoam plate.

"I'm gonna get another," Henrietta said.

"No!" Brenda latched herself on to her cousin once again and pulled her away from the concession stands. "Too much grease. You'll get zits all over your nasty ass."

"You can pop them for me like you used to."

They began to walk the circle again, and when she looked to the center all the dancers were just now mixing in. Had so little time passed? Brenda felt like she had walked onto the grounds and eaten hours ago.

The children were the final group of dancers to blend into the crowd. Even through her drunken haze she could feel the song was coming to an end. All dancers except the children stopped in unison and silence followed the echo of the last beat.

The powwow emcee's voice blared over the speakers. "Ah-hoka! Look at that beautiful Grand Entry! If you look up you can see two bald eagles soaring high!"

Brenda craned her neck and saw the black lines circling above. They always showed up at the gatherings. Because of the spiritual connection. Or because they were scavengers and they knew there would be scraps of food when everyone left. She was not a fan of eagles. Or eagle tattoos, like all three of her children's fathers had. Chris on his shoulder, and Zhaawanong across his back. Dominic also had ink, but of images rare this far north: Guadalupe, a rosary, and a golden eagle on a cactus.

"Always, in recognition of our veterans, it's time to honor the *ogichidaag* in our community with the flag song. Holding the veterans' flag for the Geshig Honor Guard is Vinny Kelliher," the emcee said.

Brenda stopped walking and stared into the center of the circle. Vincent was an old man. Short and stout with skin like wet peanut shells. Though he wasn't speaking now, he could have been heard over the crowd and the speakers. He was a man who spoke as if he had never retired from his drill-sergeant days. He had served in three wars and lived to tell the tale.

But his grandson Kayden couldn't even survive the reservation into adulthood. When Brenda saw Vinny—or any of the Kellihers—it was as if her son's trial had started all over and she could do nothing to save him again.

"Let's go," Brenda said, tugging on Henrietta's arm. "I need a drink."

Her cousin had no objections. "We can't ride the shuttle again. You know anyone here with a car?"

"Let's just walk to the Classic Shack."

Half a mile from the powwow grounds was a local watering hole, strategically placed by the non-Indian owners to make money during the summer. Most of the drunks kicked out of the grounds were either coming from or going to the Classic.

At the bar, Henrietta tried to order them another round of the disgusting beer she had given them earlier in the day.

"No," Brenda insisted. "I remember what I'm doing." She slammed one of her last three twenty-dollar bills on the counter. "Patron. No chaser."

"Just one?" the bartender asked.

"Nope."

She and her cousin clinked their glasses, took the shots, and wandered over to the gaming area. The last things Brenda remembered about her time at the Classic Shack were losing at cricket, which gave her another pint of Bud Light each time, and shutting off her cell phone at four p.m. when she was marked late for the first time in three years, and then eventually, as a no-show.

═════════

THE FIRST THINGS SHE saw when she came to were water and porcelain as hunks of whole hominy and chalky pink slime covered her toilet bowl. As her mind slowly came into focus, she remembered every awful thing and person that had led her to this place. Not just her cousin Henrietta or Kayden Kelliher's daughter.

Who she remembered first was Eunice Lafournier. The woman her parents abandoned her with for a few months. Her Good Mother. Good in the way her own mother should have been: loving, gentle, warm.

Brenda did not hate Eunice for not fighting her birth parents when they came back and took her away, but she had a hard time remembering the love she used to feel for the Lafourniers. She knew it was there, a first memory of laughs and just enough food to not go hungry, a cabin made of faded red pine. Eunice was a mother and Hazel a sister. Now Eunice was a memory underneath reservation soil and Hazel just another cousin who never bothered to check in.

The sharp taste of the mouthwash hit her tongue and almost made her spew again, but instead she began to laugh. The mouthwash was not as sharp as it could have been since she had switched to the alcohol-free variety years ago. It was her first step toward sobriety after realizing how low and desperate she had sunk, buying Listerine at the Geshig convenience because the liquor store was closed.

Just like now, she had ended up painting the toilet, only then with a minty-fresh twist. At her first AA meeting, her group leader told her she was lucky she had expelled it because she could have died.

"What if I want to?" was her response, one she recalled in shame now, even though she felt like roadkill just standing in her bathroom.

"Is that what you really feel, Brenda?" the leader said. "Tell us about it."

Quickly she had apologized but refused to elaborate on what made her say that.

Brenda stumbled from room to room in her house, switching on every light and looking for any clues. If she had found Henrietta or some other cousin on her couch—or god forbid some barfly in her bed like she might have done years ago—things might have cleared up. How she got home. When she left the Classic Shack. Where her cell phone was.

She sat on the empty couch in the living room, sipped a mug of water, and tried to clear her head. This was nothing new to her, just a few years too late and unwelcome. After a minute or an hour, she could stand up again and pace the room. On the walls were pictures of both her girls. Natalie and Tasha, and their own children.

It was the faces of her three grandchildren that had pushed her into sobriety. Natalie had one gorgeous son, Adrian, ten years old and wild. Tasha had five-year-old twin girls, Mariposa and Memengwaa. Brenda had been to each of their births, but afterward her daughters did not trust her around their children.

"I'm not going to let you do to them what you did to us," Tasha had said. "What you did to Jared."

Mother and daughter stared and each waited for the other to say something to take the sting away. In that moment, Brenda wanted to give in to anger, scream, slap her daughter like she was a little girl again, but the twins' cooing in harmony in the crib stopped her.

None of Jared's pictures were on the wall anymore. All of them were boxed away. Baby pictures. Grade school. Birthdays. She had considered giving every photo to his father or his sisters but when she had the chance to rid herself of the reminders, she could not remove the box from the house.

The only photo of Jared that mattered anymore was his mug shot.

Whatever was left in her stomach suddenly flooded to her throat and undid the work of the mouthwash. She made it to the kitchen sink before any could land on her floor. None was solid. When the heaving finally stopped and she was ready for sleep, the clock on the oven read four minutes past midnight.

In the first dream she had after passing out, she was at the prison where Jared was rotting. Kayla Kelliher's words, not her own. He was not a rot. He was her flower. But the guards at the prison would not bring him out. She sat at a gray table in a gray prison and the only color she could see was orange jumpsuits on faceless men and the guards never returned from the doors with Jared. There was nothing particularly gruesome about the dream, only that it felt like hours of waiting.

In the dream she had after waking up with a dry throat, getting a drink of water, and passing out again, she was at the tribal court. Her daughters were middle school aged again, and instead of just jumping a girl in the bathroom for her money, they killed her. The girl's family was suing Brenda for ten million dollars and the court found her guilty of raising monsters.

She did not sleep much after that, but she could still feel that teetering sway and tight clench of her inner cheeks at the back of her mouth that told her the hangover hadn't quite passed.

When she finally fell asleep mostly sober, there was no dream but a queasy yet settled peace.

———

CHUCK BIRSTON WAS KNOWN as a hard-ass manager, and he did not hesitate to fire his "problem children." The hotel was one of two departments that allowed for workers as young as sixteen, but the majority of his problem children were middle-aged, like Brenda.

It was a shock to her that she was even hired by him after her botched jobs over the years. Especially because Chuck was one of the few white managers. All of the casino's jobs were Indian preference, which generally meant leniency to fellow Indian employees. A worker could miss two days a week per month and keep their job with the right story and manager.

Brenda had neither.

She walked into the hotel with her slate-gray polo and apron, did not make eye contact with Lily, the front desk lead, clocked in as if nothing was wrong, and began to load her cart with cleaning supplies.

"When does he want to see me?" she asked Lily before she got too far into the day's work.

"After your first wing is done."

That was probably a good sign, Brenda thought. If he was planning on firing her he would just do it, but still, the graveness in Lily's usually chipper voice did not go unnoticed by her.

The rooms on the first floor were a disaster. First Monday after a powwow was always a mess, so maybe it was just her anxiety that made this round shittier than usual.

Two rooms had clogged toilets, and one bathroom had three footprints of excrement from the toilet to the bath. Were they toddler-size feet she might have been less annoyed, but these were gigantic, probably size-14 men's.

Less than two hours passed and she was done with the round. It was almost time for her break when she saw the shape of her manager appear in the doorway of the room and beckon her. He did not wait to see if she saw him or followed.

She placed a chocolate-mint candy on a pillow, made sure the corners were smoothed out just right, and then marched the cart back to the front desk slow as she could.

Three years of perfect attendance had to count for something. That was rare even among the few departments that didn't shuffle employees in and out like speed dating. She left the cart outside the front desk counter and walked into Chuck's office.

"I heard you had a wild time at Classics," Chuck said. He spoke with his eyes focused on an open file on his desk, as if she was not even there.

"Who did you hear it from?"

"I can't reveal that."

"I know. And I'm not going to deny it."

"So, as I understand it, you were drunk on the powwow grounds, during a powwow weekend, and you missed your shift because you were throwing darts. Is that what you're not going to deny?"

"Yes. I was drunk. I fucked up. I'm not going to make an excuse for myself."

Chuck closed her file and finally met her gaze. But the manager Chuck Birston was nowhere to be found between the crow's-feet. Instead, Brenda thought she could see something vaguely resembling concern.

"Are you okay?"

". . . what?"

"Are you okay? Is something going on?"

Brenda's words caught in her throat and she stared at him with utter confusion. Those were not the kinds of questions he asked, and it instantly made her uncomfortable.

"I have your attendance records for the past ten years. All the departments you worked in. The other managers really don't like you." He laughed. That was closer to his usual manner. "But it looks like you've turned things around."

"I know. I've tried really hard. It was—"

"You also attended AA a couple years ago, right?"

"Excuse me? Why the hell do you know that?"

"It's all here in your file. Information you freely gave to at least one of the managers. I'll ask again. Are you okay? Something had to have pushed you off that wagon."

She knew she could never have it in her to bring the words *I'm not okay* to her lips, her eyes weren't so tight about it. Two snail-slow tears trailed over her cheeks. "I'll never see my son again ..."

"I didn't know you had a son."

"Jared. He's gonna be thirty soon ... Do you know the Kellihers?"

"If they're a local family, I don't really. Truthfully I'm never really on this reservation except for work."

She laughed and wiped her tears. There was always that one white person at the casino who didn't know the rez and didn't care. "Jared killed a boy named Kayden. They were only seventeen. That's like, still a baby, ain't it? You remember being seventeen? I don't remember forty or thirty or even last year as much as I remember being a teenager."

"I see. So where does your absence come in?"

She rolled her eyes just as the tissue dabbed at the sides. "There's this little girl. Maya Kelliher ... I think I know more about her than my own two baby granddaughters ... She was Kayden's."

"He had a child before he died?"

Brenda shook her head and felt the stiffness of the past fifteen years creaking in her bones. "No. He never got to meet her. She was born six months after he died ... I saw her at the bar. I swear, I wasn't going to touch the booze. I never do. Ask my daughters, ask the waitresses. I never order beer ..." She decided to try to force more tears and leave Henrietta out of the story. There was a slim chance Chuck would be lenient, but zero chance if he knew she'd been drinking before the girl walked in. "But I saw Kayden's daughter. Still a baby. But starting to be a woman. Another little Indian child that doesn't know their daddy ... all because of my son ..."

She held her breath to make the sob that escaped more dramatic.

"Hmm. I see. Well, I'll have you sign this and ask you to mind your attendance from now on."

He handed her a three-layer carbon-copy document. It was a notice of a one-day suspension, date to be determined.

"... really?"

"Really, what? Call-ins on powwow weekends are automatic suspensions."

"Thank you, Mr. Birston."

"Good luck with the rest of the wing. You didn't hear it from me, but the other housekeepers gave you the worst rooms for ditching them."

She managed a laugh and stood up.

For the rest of the day, no amount of fecal matter or mysterious bed stains could bring down her sense of relief.

———

A MONTH AFTER BRENDA'S one-day bender, she brought the photos of Jared out from the basement. They were untouched by dust and in the same condition as when she packed them away. No moisture damage or fading.

Natalie and Tasha took one look at the photos and declined her offer to take them.

"I mean, why?" Tasha said. "Honestly, it's not like we know him that well."

"Yeah, Mom. I mean, do you even visit him? Neither of us have in years."

"Does that mean he's not your brother?" Brenda asked.

"I'd rather not answer that. You won't like it." Tasha still had a razor tongue.

"Okay. If you're going to be like that, then I can be like that too, right?" Brenda closed her eyes. "I don't want them right now. I don't want to get rid of them but I don't want them here."

"Are you gonna want them back? We can put them in storage or something," Natalie suggested.

Outside the children's voices shouted, some game about the small tree stumps in her yard. "I want them kept safe as possible. Can one of you please keep them?"

"Fine," Natalie said. "I'll take them. No idea where I'll find the room but I'll keep them." There was a slight petulance to her tone, the brattiness of earlier years. "Can I have a cigarette?"

She gave both of her daughters a few of her menthols, hugged them, and they left. The grandkids went with. She wanted them to stay the night for the first time in weeks, but her daughters had found out about the relapse. A promise is a promise, they said, and she would need to stay sober longer to win back their trust. Again.

Brenda sat in a mesh lawn chair and stared at her empty yard, where her grandchildren were supposed to be. Instead, there was nothing but a white propane tank, a clothesline, and undisturbed grass. The drink holder on her chair held a diet soda, and in the corner of her eye the silver can occasionally looked like a beer.

Seven

Plastique Shaman

"MAYBE YOU NEED A name."

The morning does not bring my mother back. Anni's eyes are dark red and flickering like a weathered filmstrip. He hasn't had a cup of coffee in years—even the idea of caffeine addiction makes him uncomfortable—but the smell of the fresh pot woke me up. I slept easily unlike him.

"I've made it this far without one," I say.

"Think of how much easier everything could have been." His head bobs down and shoots back up, almost rhythmically as he tries to stay awake.

"Does Hazel have a name?"

"Wiijiwaagan, my life partner," Anni says.

"That's not a name."

"Well, fine. She refused a name too. The hell made you Lafourniers so stubborn?"

When I was in middle school Ojibwe class, I first learned the concept of having an Indian name. Or spirit name. The phrase we had to use for our English name actually translates to "pretend to be called." *Marion Lafournier indizhinikaaz.* I pretend to be called Marion Lafournier.

But I've never had the feeling that I was *not* Marion. I've hated my name before, sure. Going through middle school with the nickname Mary Ann La-Four-Eyes wasn't the best, especially when I always tried to hide my sexuality but still faced some rumors anyway.

"Indians aren't complete unless they have a traditional name," my Ojibwe teacher told us in middle school. "I have two given to me by an elder. One I can share and one I keep to myself."

Anni insists that I should receive my name, that it'll stop this haunting or whatever is going on with me.

I once got a test result back from a clinic that made me celibate for months. Chlamydia of the throat. Other than feeling angry with myself on how stupid I'd been, I also felt sick and unclean. I had no symptoms but I had to spend a whole weekend before I could get antibiotics, knowing there were these nasty *things* inside me that shouldn't be there.

If what Anni says about dead bodies is true, and if it's connected to the dog and Kayden Kelliher's grave, I wonder now if there was some part of Kayden's spirit living with me all this time, like an infection sitting in my throat.

I take out a cigarette, Marlboro Red, and toss it to him. "Okay. You can name me."

He catches the cigarette on the filter between his index and middle finger tips, careful not to let the tobacco fall. "That's not how you gift *asemaa.*"

"Sorry." I try to take the cigarette back but he withholds it.

"But I'll accept it. I can't actually give you a name, but I can take you to someone who can."

I resist the urge to roll my eyes, and instead ask him if he wants me to cook him something for breakfast. The chair legs scrape across the kitchen floor and his body wilts down, asleep. I finish my coffee and then drag him to the couch.

Outside, I let the dogs out of their kennel and they take to the yard as if it was new to them again. Unlike Basil at the park, none of them seem interested in the place where the Revenant was. The youngest two mutts run off into the nearby woods, the pit bull paws at the roots of a tree, with the German shepherd circling, and Kuba plops down by my feet on the porch.

My phone still has no text or call from my mother. Anni's phone is similarly silent. His is a cheap flip phone with no service other than calls, so there's no real privacy for me to break by checking it.

Turkey Feather is a much quieter reservation than Languille Lake. The biggest town here is no bigger than Geshig, and they have only one casino instead of three. Aside from the padding steps and panting of the dogs, there is not much noise out here. The yard around me is spotless, the kitchen inside spotless, the garden free of dandelions or other pests. I can't even try to be the good son while I wait, unless I learn how to finish the sweat lodge that Anni is building in the backyard.

Just for the hell of it, I open up my dating app. There isn't much service out here but the app can be accessed through Wi-Fi. There is no one within ten miles and the closest handful of profiles have no pictures. I scroll down and see Shannon's profile now has a name: *SH*. He still doesn't have a picture but he's brave enough for initials.

I'd like to say I don't watch his profile for patterns, but I do. He loves Friday nights and early, early Sunday mornings for fucking. He goes offline after every meeting of ours. He is the only profile I have marked in my favorites.

Shannon still has no description, except the relationship status is now set to "dating." And he hasn't been online for a full day. I have to assume he means he is dating me, but that's too much to hope for from a closet case.

═══

AT THE SOUTH END of Meegwan, the hub of this reservation, there is a giant turkey statue with a stone bench at its talons. Though the largest turkey farm is white-owned, the abundance of these birds gave this reservation the honorable and dignified name: Turkey Feather.

I follow Anni's truck through Meegwan, past the statue, and farther into the reservation. On this side, the woods have faded away and now there is only open pasture and gray cages filled with turkeys, the ground more shit than soil.

Anni's medicine guy lives out here. At first, Anni was insistent we drive only one car—probably wants to talk more about spirits—but I don't like being anywhere I can't get away from on my own time. So, with a rare show of some contempt, Anni let me drive myself.

The first time I had ever gone through this reservation it surprised me. Because of the abundance of trees in Geshig, I had just assumed all Ojibwes only ever lived in the woods. Out here, though, it's miles of open land with the occasional copse of trees. I follow Anni's truck nearly ten miles through backroads until I come across the house.

While driving around this state, and a few others years ago, I noticed there is always *that* house, that *one* house in every county background. It's surrounded by fields. White, two-story, with a long driveway and a station wagon out front. A perfect oak tree off to the side of the house, tire swing optional. Timeless in a way, like it would fit in any county's history-in-photographs book. It's probably in the same location in every plat map in the country. That's the house that Anni brings me to.

Except instead of an oak tree, there is a sweat lodge. It's a big dome, about the size of one storage unit, and covered in a pale tan canvas. Nearby is a small flickering firepit surrounded by rocks. Anni parks next to the owner's station wagon and I park behind it in case he wants to leave before me.

We both step outside and wait. I expect the guy to walk out of the sweat lodge wearing all buckskin but instead he walks out the front door in flannel and jeans.

It's hard not to react to the sight. This guy is like an Indian Grim Reaper. His skin is coarse, dark brown with liver spots like a loaf of raisin bread. Tufts of white hair hang out from a navy baseball cap like out-turned pockets. He smiles, but the few teeth he has left are toffee brown and do nothing to improve the unsettling look.

The eyes are the worst. Clearly bloodshot, but the whites are more like yellows, only visible at the edges of his giant irises. They look like they dried out years ago and he covered them in layers of clear nail polish to hold them in. If I met this man anywhere else, I would assume my time had come.

"*Aaniin, noozhis.*"

His voice is as friendly as any Indian grandpa's. "I'll leave you to it ..." Anni shakes the man's hand and walks inside. I assume he's going to fall asleep or watch the ball game.

The old man approaches me slowly, a regular walk that doesn't hold any sign of age. I expect him to offer a handshake but he waits.

"Oh! Right, um, here ya go." I hand him a bag of cherry-scented tobacco that Anni had at his house. "My stepfather told me a phrase to say in Ojibwe but I'll be honest, I completely spaced it out."

"That's okay, *noozhis*. He told me a little about why you're here." The man pulls out a phone from his pocket and reads a text message. It's a smartphone. Even more technologically advanced than Anni's.

"I didn't catch your name, sir."

"Ask me then."

"What's your name?"

"In Ojibwe. Try '*Aaniin ezhinikaazoyan?*'"

"Oh yeah, sorry. *Aaniin ezhinikaazoyan?*"

"My colonial name is Carey. Ataage *indizhinikaaz.*"

"Okay." My Ojibwe may be rusty, but I believe he said *Ataage is my traditional name.*

"No use wasting time," he says as he takes off his hat and starts to undo the buttons on his flannel. "Young Aanakwad tells me you have some *maji-manidoo* following you."

I suppose a guy that looks like Carey could call anyone young. "Yeah, a ghost or a zombie, something like that."

Carey starts to laugh and fully remove his shirt. "Children

always have the biggest imagination. Ghosts aren't real, *noozhis*. That's white-people shit. What you've seen is a *manidoo*."

"Um ..."

"You're not undressing," he says. "I hope you're not uncomfortable. The young bucks today all seem to live inside their clothes like turtles."

I pull my shirt off without hesitation. "Trust me. I have no problem taking my clothes off in front of men."

I stand there naked as he carefully places a basket of hot rocks inside the sweat lodge, next to a small fire in the center. He gestures for me to join just as he pours water over the rocks from a faded ice cream bucket. The steam fills the dim enclosure and instantly my skin is slick and warm, like a humid summer night washing over me all at once, except there's no tent, river, or ex-boyfriend.

Carey sits with his legs spread as if advertising, but I know attraction when I see it and this is not it. This is just a man of another time, no shame or fear of his own parts. I sit with my legs crossed. Not out of shame but because the floor of this sweat lodge is just old pine boughs that become soft and muddy as the steam slicks every inch it can waft into.

"I'll begin with a prayer." Carey begins an invocation in Ojibwe and sprinkles tobacco over the fire in rhythm with his vocal emphasis. His eyes close but I just sit there and wait. The heat inside the lodge is building and I can feel my own sweat joining the mist, like a sauna after a night in a hot tub.

"Have you ever sat and listened to nature?" Carey asks.

"No."

"Do you pray?"

"No."

"Do you prefer white men or Indian men in your bed?"

"Um. That's a little private, isn't it?"

"We're naked."

"Even so … Why does it matter?"

"Might explain why you think so much like a white man." He laughs. "No Ojibwe name, no prayers. I can feel it in your energy. You don't respect me or this ceremony."

I shrug. "You got me there."

"Why?"

"I don't know—I guess—maybe I'd like to know a little bit about your qualifications? Do you have a degree in medicine?"

"Even better. I'm a card-carrying member of the Board of Shamans. BS for short." Carey pulls out a card from a bison-skin wallet. "Proof."

"This is a strip of birch bark." I turn it over. "And you drew a cock on it!"

"You have what the white folks call a lack of faith." Carey laughs. "You're gonna need to trust me."

"What do Indians call a lack of faith?"

"Being white."

Carey begins to rattle on for what I think is about fifteen minutes. I can't really tell because the heat of the lodge is finally getting to me. My breathing is hot and dry, like I'm sitting inside the onset of a fever. I feel my eyes closing, but I make myself sit up straight and listen to his spiel.

"Our people knew that every living thing has a spirit. And when the white men in lab coats looked in their microscopes, they found out humans and animals and plants all share the same kind of stuff in their bodies. Atoms, and carbons. Or what we called spirit. So, you see, Indians knew the truth about the world before any white scientist."

"That all sounds fascinating, but I don't feel too good."

"You're opening up your mind!" He raises his arms and looks toward the ceiling. "Let the spirits take you away!"

"I need a drink. Do you have any soda?"

"Tough it out, kid. Be a real Indian. *Ogichidaa*. I know it when I see it, *gwiiwizens*. You're a warrior. Like me."

"You don't look like a warrior. You look like a dried potato." Did I say that out loud? I really can't tell anymore; the heat is too intense.

The old man stared right into my steam-cooked eyes and sat forward. "Do you want to know the finest act of my life? My defining moment as an Ojibwe warrior."

"I guess."

"I blew up Mount Rushmore."

I laugh, and the dryness of my mouth causes it to spurt out like a broken squeak toy. "What?"

"I defaced that ugly rock forever. Would you like to hear that story before we talk about your name?"

"I got nowhere else to be." I feel my head and shoulders rock back and forth. This feeling…it's not all that different from being baked out of my fucking mind. A ringing starts inside my ears, like I can feel the shape of the canals and the eardrums pulsing with the steam. And then the only thing I can hear is Carey's voice.

I looked up at those faces and thought, fuck, these white rats are ugly. Great White Fathers? Good thing us apples fell far from the tree. I was with AIM back then.

The American Indian Movement?

Yes, gwiiwizens. I knew all those guys. But I had to prove myself because I had just recently come back from 'Nam. That's where I learned how to make bombs.

What kind of bomb did you make?

A small one. Like the size of a cherry. I thought it would be funny lighting a cherry bomb on Slave Master Washington's cunt face. Anyway, I had to prove myself to the honchos in charge so I whipped up a bomb, brought it right to the tip-top of the mountain and I lit it. At first I tried to run away, but when I looked back and saw the wick shrinking, I knew this was how I wanted to go out. I wanted to ride the crumbles of these white rats all the way down until I was crushed to death. I'd be a hero for the ages.

But you didn't do it.

Of course I did, gwiiwizens! I just survived, and then ran away before the park rangers could arrest me.

That's a neat story. Except for the part where Mount Rushmore is still there, but, ya know, a good story.

Carey's eyes bore into mine with cherry-red lines on the yellowing whites. "So, you've been there? You've been to Mount Rushmore and know it's there?"

"No. But—"

"Then how do you know it's there?"

"Because . . . I mean, it's not exactly something you can hide. I don't buy into conspiracy theories."

"Ah. So that's what you're taking from this, you can only trust what you see with your own eyes?"

"I don't feel good. You sure you don't have like a Sprite or a Heineken in here?"

"Tell me what you saw. Again. Tell me what you saw."

I try to speak but my throat is burning, and the headache has spread all across my forehead and through my eyes. "I saw a dog. It came back to life from underneath some playground equipment. And it led me to Kayden Kelliher's grave."

"Why?"

"I don't know!"

"Why?" he shouts.

"I don't fucking know, asshole!"

"Why?" His scream echoes across the sweat lodge like a cannon and then his voice changes. His mouth moves but it's not his voice. The dead marble eyes glower like a spinning nickel. *"There are four. Worlds. The Ojibwe walk in. But it is not. You. That is walking now."*

Fuzzy orange lights overtake my eyes and I run out of the sweat lodge. My tongue tastes the sour green grass before my lungs begin to heave and I throw up a rancid mix of bile and coffee.

After a few minutes of suffering, I feel a jet of moisture across my face. Above me, the medicine man is holding a garden hose and spraying it right into my face.

"You need to sweat more. Like a real Indian."

I snatch the hose from him and inhale as much as I can without drowning myself.

———

THE WOULD-BE MEDICINE MAN can't make a good cup of coffee.

Inside his house Anni and I are eating bowls of potato soup

with specks of disintegrated corned beef. His coffeepot needs a cleaning, for the taste resembles a mix between burned bread and a mouthful of coins. I remember when I was a kid, pennies tasted the worst.

Anni and Carey are talking about the Vikings season while I sit in silence and wait for words to form. I really can't speak. It feels like there is a chain-lock on my throat whenever I think I have something to say. The creamy soup is helping but the coffee seems to reset the progress.

I finish the last bite and take a breath. "Did you shop at Jake's Hot Springs or Northern Spa Solutions?"

Carey throws his head back and a laugh like a backfiring car spurts from his throat. "Jake's. They offered a better interest rate. How could you tell?"

Back in the sweat lodge, while he was going on about spirits or some shit, I noticed a logo on the side of the benches. It was the logo of a line of spas that rich white people buy to host swinger parties or just because they're bored with their disposable income, I guess.

I know this because I sat in a similar sauna and hot tub when a pair of older married men invited me over, gave me champagne, and relived their wild days of youth all over my body. Really makes me question that degree in BS Carey claimed he had.

"I'm building my own house," I reply. "Thinking about what kind of spa I'm gonna put in it."

Anni knows I'm lying but he knows me well enough to just nod.

"Well, ya got me. I cut a few corners, but no one should lose faith over it. I am still willing to dream your name, *noozhis.*"

"*Miigwech*. You can just text it to me when you find it."

Carey begins a retort but just then my cell phone rings. The screen lights with Shannon's scruffy face. He never calls, so this must be important.

I excuse myself and answer.

"What's going on?" No use pretending that something isn't wrong. "Is Basil okay?"

"I'm sorry, Marion." Shannon's voice is flatter than usual. "I—I can't find him."

"Okay. How did that happen?"

I feel guilty that what he says next affects me more than knowing Basil is gone.

"My—uh. My girlfriend let him outside this morning. She didn't think he'd run away."

"I'll be back today."

"Marion, I'm s—"

I hang up the phone and take a deep breath. The red eyes of the Revenant stare into mine again, this time in my stupor from the sweat lodge. Other images flash, ones I couldn't have ever seen before. A cabin made of red pine. A young girl drinking liquor while her sisters watch.

A gaunt and tough-faced woman, putting pieces of food on a blackened jawbone.

I text Shannon. *Meet me at my place in two hours. I know exactly where he is.*

Eight

The Lost Forty

Hazel

GOOD MOTHERS DON'T GIVE their sons marijuana.

Great ones do.

Hazel repeated this in her mind over and over as she drove away from Marion and the house she and Anni shared. It boiled down to simple actions that her body knew even when cloudy.

Open door.

Sit down.

Seat belt.

Keys in ignition.

Leave it all behind.

The Famous Disappearing Act of Hazel Lafournier.

Except she knew in the cerulean-moonlit road that she would turn back.

Stop the car.

Let it idle.

Stare into the woods.

Light another joint.

And then she would return to wake the dogs and explain to Marion and Anni why she drove off. Again. How long had it been since her last incident? Not anytime recent. Not since her marriage and since Marion moved out for the first time.

It must have been at least ten years, maybe two years after Kayden's death. It couldn't have been right after because she never would have abandoned Kayla in her time of grief, but it was definitely when Marion was in high school.

Was he mad? She could not remember.

It seemed like something that should be simple to recall. Was a teenage boy mad at his mother leaving?

No. When Marion

was a teenager he

spent his days in his room

listening to sad music and pretending.

On the road ahead of her, the coarse gray of the reservation roads began to turn into a more smooth, slick black. Hazel reached the highway, lit another joint.

And she left again.

═══════

THE HIGHWAY OUT OF the reservation that led to Fargo began in a series of wide curves and a few small lakes and resorts. Hazel knew the roads well enough to drive in any condition.

Drunk.

High.

Crying because of her mother's death.

Crying after her best friend's son's death.

Crying because the smoke
filled the car and began
to sting her eyes.

She opened the windows and the smoke dissipated. Her cell
phone rang. Either Anni or Marion, but she did not answer.

The winding roads eventually flattened out and the highway
to Fargo was just one left turn away, a smooth drive with only a
handful of traffic lights, little chance of getting stopped by a cop
this time of night.

Only, she did not know whether to turn left or right. She had
no idea where she was going to, but she did know that she had
options.

She could turn right and visit Kayla Kelliher in Geshig. Or
Brenda Haltstorm. The two women she never thought she would
leave behind.

She could turn left and find wherever Jamison lived in Fargo.
Finally tell him to his face about his firstborn son.

She could turn around and rejoin Anni and Marion, pretend
she had never left.

But they knew, and she knew more than anyone, that once a
person leaves their life behind, however temporarily, there is no
apology that will wipe it away. Hazel and Eunice would always
be the mothers who left.

No, that's not true, she knew. They weren't like she had been
to her mother, vicious, resentful, unforgiving. She could be gone

for days and Anni and Marion wouldn't hate her. It was she who had the problem with leaving, both forgiving her mother and forgiving herself.

The eyes of the wolf had caused her to leave, and now the headlights approaching in the mirror behind her hastened her decision.

Left

   Right

Left

   Right

Simple as that, she told herself. Simple as that.

========

SHE WANTED TO WALK out on her second baby's life because her first had walked out on her. Or rather, he stopped breathing and then left her body without a goodbye. Jamison would have talked her out of it upon her first doubt. Had he known she was pregnant again.

"Did you know some Ojibwe can see the future?" he said the night they met, with a big smile full of dark, tobacco-stained teeth. "I see a lot of you in mine."

Now she sat in an empty apartment and wished she had never inflicted herself onto that man's future in any way.

Hazel met Jamison Reyes not long after her twenty-first birthday at a dive bar in Minneapolis. She and a friend from work were shooting pool and tequila and two women alone in a bar were bound to attract some kind of attention. She was not really looking for a man's attention, but when Jamison gave it to her she seemed to crave it like a fresh pack of cigarettes. The day after, when she woke up in his bed with no memory of the night before, he claimed he saved her from starting a bar brawl with a group of white college girls.

From the moment he first challenged her to a game of eight ball, her impulse to clash was always met. They fought harder and with more vitriol and passion than she and her mother, Eunice, ever had. She had never known a man worthier of fighting with than Jamison, or of making love with, or walking with, driving with, smoking weed with, anything two people in love could do.

Jamison was a fast-moving man and within the first month of dating Hazel he was convinced that he needed everything she could give. He wanted her hate as much as her love, and he wanted to bind her to himself as quickly as he could.

"Indian chicks are the craziest bitches out there," Jamison quipped one night while pretending to be more drunk than he was. "They'll just fight you! Won't even think twice to punch their man."

Hazel knew where the sentiment came from. Eunice was not an easy woman to deal with, let alone be raised by, and many of her cousins were on track to become the same kind of woman in their sunset years. "I know what you mean," she told him. Then she punched him in the face.

Her small hand had somehow left a large bruise on his temple, and it did not satisfy her like she thought it would. Her blood still splashed under the skin of her ears and cheeks, and the anger kept down her fear of the retaliation. Give a punch, take a punch. It was only fair, she thought.

Jamison refused to hit her. He sank into the couch and stared at her as if he was waiting for an apology and a kiss. Hazel realized then that it was a ploy; he would never hit her and she now had the guilt of being the violent one. The only touch he gave her was a soft caress of her stomach. Later, she did not know if Jamison had actually said it or if it was something she imagined.

"It's time ..."

One month later, Hazel was pregnant, and desperately wishing Jamison had returned that punch. Then she could have left with no guilt.

———

MONTHS AFTER SHE HAD left him, Hazel received a drunken phone call. He was back up on their reservation and trying to marry the first woman who would let him into her bed.

I'm going to have a great life without you, Hazel. You're garbage. You deserve the cities.

Hazel hadn't given much thought to what she deserved. She had survived her mother's rolling-stone lifestyle after they left Geshig behind, and she made it through her rebellious phase without many scars. She still smoked weed way more than she should, but her life was never a true mess until now.

She loved Jamison. She even missed him sometimes. Their relationship was always what she saw her family members have, so it felt right. Normal. Their children would have no trouble with enrollment because of their shared blood quantum. And she ran away from all that a few months after her miscarriage.

Both of them had been so devastated when it happened that they never discussed trying again. Instead, they just grew silent and distant with each other. Or perhaps that was just her. But after she had moved out and he left to heal the wounds in reservation bars, she couldn't help but wonder if her second pregnancy was intentional.

The first time she thought about getting an abortion was easy. She had never truly wanted a child before, so why not? The only people who would try to stop her didn't know she was pregnant.

The second time she thought about abortion, she began to make up ridiculous things to convince herself otherwise. What if this baby is meant to be? What if he's meant to change the world? Why is it a he now?

The third and last time was after she told her best friend, Kayla, who she had grown apart from after leaving the reservation. Kayla was in the middle of raising her own toddler and was adamant that Hazel should keep the baby.

"I don't have the money for that, Kayla. I can barely afford rent now."

"I still don't understand why you moved to the cities in the first place. You never had to pay rent up here."

"Yeah, but that means I'd still be living with that woman, and I just can't anymore."

"Oh Hazel, you hold too much anger inside. If I could talk to my mother again ..."

"Yeah, yeah, guilt trip noted and ignored. You know how Eunice is, I just couldn't deal."

"Well, how about you move in with me again? No rent. At least for a while until you get your bearings up here. I bet I could get you in with the tribe."

"Oh no. Never going back to Languille Lake again. Not as long as Eunice and Jamison are there."

Kayla went silent for three seconds before she said "Oh. So you haven't heard."

Hazel's breath caught in her throat. Could Jamison have drunk himself to death already? Would she be relieved or saddened? "Probably not, if you think I haven't. Tell me!"

"Jamison enlisted. He's in South Carolina for training."

"Why the hell do you know that and I don't?"

"You underestimate reservation gossip."

Now Hazel went silent. She took a breath. "I'll call you back soon, I promise. Bye."

She sat down, held her stomach, and thought about the father she had never met. Laverne Graycalm. Dead at thirty, widowed, and no legacy except his house on Lake Anders where Eunice still lived. Now her own child's father, probably off to war. It hadn't even been over a year since Desert Storm ended, maybe he wouldn't be in danger ... but the jawbone.

Bullhead had passed away well before Hazel was born, but Eunice told the story of the jawbone like it was the Nativity. She wasn't superstitious but couldn't help but wonder if Jamison would be the next in a long line of men destroyed by their Lafournier Indian women.

His drunken message was still on her answering machine.

Hazel had already destroyed his life. She held her stomach and wondered if she could really do it now.

One day later, Hazel called Kayla back and said the words she never thought she'd have to say again.

"I'm ... I'll do it. I'll come live with you in Geshig. But the moment you do that dumb sitcom thing where you try to get me and Eunice to talk, I'm kicking both of your asses and leaving."

"I knew you'd come back, girlfriend! You're going to love Kayden! He's such a handful but he's talking now and he—"

Hazel set the phone on the counter and let her friend prattle about her son. Would she turn into that if she really had this baby? What about Jamison? What would happen if he survived? Maybe he wouldn't come back to Geshig.

She sighed, picked up the phone, said goodbye, and hung up.

It was a hopeless thought that she'd never see Jamison again. She knew as she packed her bag that he would be back. Everyone, even her, comes back to Geshig.

—————

RIGHT.

Just before the car behind her approached, Hazel decided she would turn right. Not to Geshig, not to Kayla or Brenda, and *definitely* not to Jamison. But somewhere else.

But it would be a job that required daylight, so instead of driving straight to her destination, she went to her son's house in Half Lake. The paranoid boy of hers had given her an extra key in case of emergencies, and a high drive in the middle of the night seemed to her like it would fit the definition.

The kiddo's house smelled like too many Glade PlugIns or Walmart potpourri. She didn't want to invade his privacy any more than she was already doing, so she fell asleep on the couch. When she woke, it was around six a.m. and her phone was filled with missed calls and messages. Just before she could reply, the phone flashed one last breath of life and then died.

Hazel shrugged and decided to let them worry. If it got more attention from both her son and husband, no real harm was done. She left Marion's house and then went to the nearest open fast food joint in Half Lake, a remodeled McDonald's in the same lakeshore location she had visited throughout her childhood and later adulthood when she smoked too much and took late-night drives with Marion.

The food was disgusting as ever, but it helped ground her and settle her stomach as she drove through the small, waking city and made for the north highway exit. In a half hour she was near a city called Blackduck and then, after, a desolate town called Alvwood, where the only sign of life was a bar. Beyond Alvwood for another twenty-minute drive was the place she was looking for. A scientific and natural area called the Lost Forty.

Or as her grandmother had called it, the Ghost Acres.

Eunice

"PARDON ME FOR CUSSIN' in front of a lady, but that's a load of bullshit," Laverne said. "None of that was true."

Eunice laughed and took a drink of her beer. Laverne had asked her where she came from, and she told him the story her mother had always stuck with. Awaazisii, the Bullhead, living alone in the Ghost Acres with her two children by a white man. Until one day, salvation in the form of a half-French, half-Ojibwe man named Lafournier.

"Ask my cousins," Eunice said. "The Bullheads. Maybe you know some of them."

"Bullhead, bullshit. You're bluffin', little lady." Laverne spoke in a drawl he had learned from watching pictures in Minneapolis. No matter how much he pretended to be a cowboy, he couldn't hide his Swedish features, the hazel-green eyes, sandy hair, and sweetheart lips that were trying hard to impress Eunice. "Indians always think they know the real story. It's cute."

"You can find truth in any story, Laverne." She leaned in closer and brushed her hand over his knee for just a moment. "Like how Indian women aren't afraid to get what they want."

"Darlin', you are crazy. I like crazy."

"Blame my mother."

Eunice was a part-time alcoholic, and her first shift started in 1958 when she was twelve. Her older sisters Gwendoline and Shirley snuck liquor from their father and tricked her into drinking it by saying it was maple syrup.

The first sip was sweet but only for a moment. Her throat closed at the bitter taste, but she managed to keep it down, and heard their laughter. "Keep drinking. The maple is near the bottom!"

"It tastes like pine sap!" Another cruel act of theirs. Eunice had always felt stupid after falling for their tricks. Not long before, they had convinced her the sticky gray clumps on the red pine bark was candy. They made up for her anger by being the sweetest older sisters for the space of a day, and then it was back to torment. Eunice had tried to stop when the liquor began to hurt but they made her drink more and more until she couldn't stand up.

They laughed at her, and then Eunice laughed. She cried

and laughed until she felt her body sink to the cabin floor and roll around on the dried-out planks. "I'm telling! Papa! Mama!"

The girls hadn't expected their mother to burst into the cabin so quickly. Bullhead and Tomas Lafournier usually spent the whole day working in the woods, but that day they came back early, as if sensing their daughters were up to something malicious.

It took only one look at her drunken baby for Bullhead to fly into a rage. She grabbed Gwendoline and Shirley by their hair, dragged them to wall, and pushed them to their knees. Eunice kept her mouth shut as she watched her mother beat the girls' bare asses with a thin cane.

She wanted to laugh at her sisters for getting the punishment they deserved, but the words coming from her mother's mouth were a mix of Ojibwe and some English swear words. Eunice knew that if her mother was using English, she was furious. Instead of feeling saved from their torment, Eunice began to feel guilty for their welts and bruises. It felt like a weakness, and as soon as the girls spotted it, they used it every chance they could.

After their parents' deaths, Eunice, the responsible and sober child, was deeded the red pine cabin, but she never felt like she owned it. She watched both sisters turn into alcoholics, wives, mothers, and somehow, she was the one who always felt bad for their trespasses against her. Gwen and Shirley rarely failed to get what they wanted, a few cigarettes here, dollars there, a place to crash, and free babysitting whenever they decided to clock out for a few weeks.

Their hold on her began to wane when Eunice turned

twenty. Spring had finally arrived in Geshig after a winter of raising her sister's children, and at pace with the budding green, she began to leave the house. Her oldest niece Delores watched the other children and Eunice drove to the only bar in Geshig that would serve Indians.

"So let's say I believe ya." Laverne grabbed a few strands of her hair and braided it. The weave was nice, but it annoyed Eunice that he did not ask. "Does that mean you're gonna kill me in the night and steal our children away?"

"You got me." She pushed his dainty hands away from her hair. "That's my big plan. Steal your name, your kids, and your house. Far as I see it, you cowboys have it coming."

"You'll have to get my hand in marriage first, darlin'." When he smiled, she saw his teeth, slightly hidden by the shadow of his big, sweetheart lips, and wondered for a moment if she should walk away.

"I'll try my best."

=====

ONE YEAR AFTER THEIR marriage, and only six months after his draft, a pair of soldiers came to Laverne's front door. Eunice held her stomach as they handed her a folded flag and told her that her husband was now nothing more than a spray of red across a lush, green forest.

Another dead husband. Eunice silently cursed her mother Bullhead for losing the jawbone, and then held the flag to her heart. But she shed no tears. Never for a white man.

From that moment, Eunice became a full-time alcoholic, and her only child by Laverne lived the consequences.

Hazel

THE SCENIC AREA HAD an honor system. There was a brown tin box on a signpost that said FEES and it was expected that everyone who explored the Lost Forty would pitch in at least fifteen dollars.

This was my family's land, Hazel reasoned with herself. I don't have to pay a dime.

She walked onto the trails, and the first step took her into the world her mother had often spoken of.

The trails were narrow and winding, each dip with a natural formation of stairs from the giant tree roots. The underbrush between the trees was lush, green, and prickly, with some wisps of color scattered around. Pink and yellow lady's slippers grew in abundance, along with sun-yellow tulips and small daisies.

At the end of the main trail, beneath a big row of a tree root staircase, there was a damp, north-facing plank that led out into the lake that gave this place life in more ways than one. It fed the banks, and the mistake of marking the entire area as a lake saved it from the lumberjacks. Hazel walked onto the plank just until the tips of her toes touched the water. She knelt and swished her fingertips inside the mucky waves, and then rinsed off the grime and dried her hands on her jeans.

The wind blew southward and Hazel turned around. From the bank, she looked up and could see each of the trees of the Lost Forty and knew where she had to go.

Underneath the largest red pine in the state, with lines of bark like an old man's skin, Hazel found a small area of soft soil just between two of the roots. She looked around, made sure no one was obviously watching, and then began to dig.

It was hard at first, getting the dirt to move away from the knotted, ancient roots, but once the top layer was gone the easier it became to search. She dug down beneath the roots for nearly a foot before she felt it.

A cold, hard half ring of bumpy ridges. She pulled it from the earth and held it in her arms like a newborn. The jawbone. Buried with Bullhead's ashes, just like Eunice always claimed her father had done.

Eunice

GLASS SHATTERED, AND A rock the size of a fist bounced across the cabin floor. Eunice stumbled to the front door and saw Hazel running toward the road. She waited at the porch, but her daughter did not come back. Until evening she stayed there, her intoxication sinking with the sun, and then she went back inside.

There was no electricity, and the cabin was a mess. No one had been there to take care of it since god knew how long. Eunice didn't care. She grew up without constant warmth, but Hazel was born in a better time. She was as fragile as children could be in this world that was leaving Eunice behind, just like it left Tomas and Bullhead. The world was always leaving Indians in the dust.

Eunice began to think about all the times in the past four years that she had made Hazel move to a different city with her and then back to Geshig. She only felt guilty about dragging her daughter across the state when she was sober, so like any good mother would do, she never stopped drinking. And Hazel never stopped hating it.

In the stale, foggy morning, Eunice drove around Geshig looking for her teenage daughter. She was not in any of the obvious places, not with Gwen or Shirley, not even with the Haltstorms. Instead, Eunice found her in the back of the library reading old copies of the *Geshig Herald*.

"I don't wanna leave," Hazel said.

"I thought you hated it here."

"I hate it everywhere. I hate the cities. I hate the cabin. You never let me stay long enough to love them."

It was the saddest thing she had ever heard. Sadder than poor Brenda's cries at being kidnapped by her own father. The only home Hazel had known was now a dump, broken beyond repair.

"If you're not gonna leave, are you gonna stay at the cabin?"

"No."

"Then what should we do?"

"You do what you want. Leave me alone."

Like a good mother, Eunice listened to her.

It took less than an hour for Eunice to find a home for her. She went right to the tribal council office from the library, still hungover from the whiskey, and asked for Georgina Kelliher.

"She doesn't work here anymore," the young woman at the reception desk said.

"Do you have her address or phone number maybe?"

"I ain't an operator, lady. I can't give that shit out or forward you to her, jeez."

"Well then . . ." Eunice leaned forward and stared into the girl's face. She sighed and let her whiskey breath wash over her.

"What can you do for me? The tribal council is supposed to serve the tribe and I'm part of the tribe."

"Ugh. You fuckin' reek, lady!"

"My name is Eunice Lafournier, and I know I reek." Eunice thought about the sad cries of her daughter. "Do you happen to have any job openings too?"

The receptionist stood up and walked away. "Yeah, yeah, I'll put you on the list. Hang on."

Not five minutes later, the recognizable face of Lindale Kelliher came out to the reception area. "Eunice? Hello! Are you back in Geshig permanently?"

"I don't know yet, Mr. Kelliher. I'm not in the best situation at the moment." The young woman stared at her with a smug face, eager to hear some gossip no doubt. "Can we talk in private?"

"Are you having some trouble?" he said, beckoning her back to his office.

"Yes. It's my daughter ..." The door to the office shut. "I have a big favor to ask you."

———

ON THE WAY BACK to the cabin, Hazel now placated at the thought of living with the Kelliher family, Eunice choked back tears while giving her daughter whatever she could muster for advice.

"The Kellihers are proud. You have to be polite, be careful with every word you say."

"I know what they're like, Eunice."

Hazel wouldn't take her eyes away from the window, which

was better for Eunice because her daughter didn't see her wince at the tone with which she said her name. "I got no advice for you about boys. The war may be over, but that draft could come back any day so be careful who you give your heart to."

"Can you just stop talking?"

"If war don't get them, something will. All goes back to my mom and that jawbone of hers. Remember that, Hazel. Whoever's face that bone belonged to, he don't like us Lafourniers and Bullheads being happy."

"Jesus Christ, Mom, it's not the old west anymore! No one believes in curses or powwows or any of your parents' bullshit!"

Eunice stayed quiet for the rest of the car ride, said nothing when Hazel gathered her few belongings from the red pine cabin, and nothing else all the way to the Kellihers' place east of Geshig.

Before her daughter left the car and left her life behind, Eunice grabbed her shoulder and held her back. "Call us crazy, we're used to it. But the moment a boy with sweet lips gives you a black-toothed smile, just know there's nothing you can do to save him. I love you, kiddo, now go on and get off to your new family."

=====

HAZEL BROUGHT THE CURSED bones down to the plank and began to wash away the soil. It fell away easy as dandruff and what was left only vaguely resembled what she had pictured as a girl. The bones were dark brown, as if made from ebony, and where there should have been nothing but space there was a layer of solid rock. Bullhead must have mounted the jawbone to some kind of clay base.

That, or the jawbone was a fake, and had always been a fake, a bedtime story to teach the children a lesson.

Real or fake, Hazel left the Ghost Acres without looking back and held the jawbone in her hands like a trophy.

Nine

Red Pine

CAREY PROMISED ME HE would be in touch if he dreams my name. I feigned interest but really, if his magic dreams do work and he finds my "true name" he can keep it. Right now, as I drive away from Turkey Feather and back toward Languille Lake, there's only one thing I care about.

Not Basil. I do care about him, but I'm not worried about it. He'll be fine.

When I'm agitated, sometimes I don't take notice of my surroundings as I drive and it feels like no time has passed even though one hundred miles later I'm pulling back into my driveway in Half Lake. Shannon's truck is waiting on the street.

"You really wanna date a woman that can't take care of a dog?" I say as he steps out. He is wearing a dark red flannel shirt and tight blue jeans.

"Shut the fuck up, Marion. Just stop. We can fight after you show me where your dog is." He takes off his sunglasses, revealing bloodshot eyes, and rubs his temples. "Ya know, I don't believe you. There's a thousand places he could be on the rez and you just automatically think you know where he went?"

"Yeah, he's my dog. Of course I know."

"You're such a fuckin' asshole!"

"Why?"

He throws his arms up and shakes his head. "You just don't even care. Supposedly you love your dog, he runs away, and you don't give a shit."

I start to laugh, which doesn't impress him. "I'm not worried because I know exactly where he is. If you don't believe me, follow me and find out. And if he's not there, then your girlfriend can buy me a new dog."

"Just get in." He rolls his eyes and doesn't say another word. I get in his truck and try to hide my smile.

I'm annoyed at him for hiding the girlfriend and not telling me. I'm upset, I can't hide that. But it's useless wasting the energy in being mad, so instead I decide to tease him.

"Did you tell her it was your boyfriend's dog she lost?"

He says nothing and puts his sunglasses back on.

"Does she know you like to suck cock?"

I expect some show of anger, but instead he just turns the radio up and focuses on the road ahead of him. We travel nearly halfway to Geshig before I can't handle the silence.

"Okay, okay, I'm sorry. Can you turn down the music so we can talk?" In the few times I've been inside this truck, whether it was for sex or not, I've been afraid to touch anything inside of it except the seat belt and buckle.

Shannon turns down the music and sighs. "I'm already nibbling by bringing you there, but I'll bite more. How the hell is it that you think you know where your damn dog is?"

Now seems like as good a time as any to hit him with the truth. Though he is initially confused about where I choose to start the story, it's truly where all this begins.

In the 1890s, a man of French descent named Baptiste Lafournier bought a small tract of woodland from the First Geshig Bank and held a mortgage with them until just shy of his death, at which point the ownership went to his only non–blood related son, Tomas Lafournier.

There's an interesting abstract of title by a local titling company that shows all this, although I think the average person might not use that word to describe mortgages.

When Baptiste was an older widower with two children already out of the house, he saved a baby from a nearby house fire that claimed the lives of Sophie and Homer Haltstorm. Baptiste adopted the baby Tomas and later let him claim the name Lafournier as his own.

So, the mortgage papers show that Baptiste passed down his land and the hand-built red pine cabin to Tomas, but later Tomas added a woman named Sophie Bullhead to the deed. Sophie wasn't her real name. My grandmother Eunice told me that her mother only ever went by Awaazisii, or Bullhead to those who couldn't say it, but she needed a legal name to marry Tomas and qualify for certain enrollee benefits.

When Bullhead died, Tomas brought her ashes back to her home up by Blackduck and not long after, he himself died and left everything to Eunice.

The red pine cabin deteriorated over the years, going from wood to tar paper by the time my mother was born. It's almost like the more Indian the ownership became, the worse it got in condition.

I explain all this to Shannon, who just nods impatiently until we are close to our destination. The Quarry Way cemetery, where all of my family is buried. And just shy of a half mile from the spot where Tomas's cabin stood.

"So, what does all that have to do with your dog?"

"I had a vision of the cabin in a sweat lodge." Even I start laughing at that. "I have no further explanation besides I really think this is where I need to go."

"Since when do you go to the sweat lodge? You told me before that you thought Indian beliefs were stupid."

"I did not!"

"That's the exact word you used. *Stupid.*"

"Oops. Well, maybe they're not. I went there because of—" I almost don't tell him because of how crazy I'm already sounding. "Because of Kayden Kelliher."

The rows of headstones come into view and Shannon parks on the grass, away from the rows at a respectful distance. He stares at me and rubs his fingernails through his greasy stubble. "You mentioned him before. Why?"

Instead of telling him directly, I open the door, jump out of the truck, and smile. "Come find out."

Without waiting to see if he follows, I lead the way past the rows of dead family and onto a small trail into the nearby woods. I hear his footsteps behind me on the crunching leaves, but I don't turn back. I wait for him to catch up and speak.

"Did you know Kayden?" he asked.

"Barely. Our mothers were best friends but I was always too young and shy to have playdates or whatever. I hated basketball and that's all he ever did when we went over."

"So, you remember him?"

"Kind of? Maybe in a forced kind of way, like, I know for a fact we went to his house a lot so it just makes sense that I would've seen him there but I don't remember ever talking or playing with him specifically."

"What's he got to do with this then? He's dead."

"Officially, yes. But I'm not so sure he's gone."

Before I can explain, we walk into the clearing where the cabin used to be.

"Are you fucking serious?" Shannon's doubts have been smacked upside the head.

Basil is sleeping right in the middle of the clearing. And just a foot away, as if holding vigil, is the Revenant.

"This is why you should never question me," I chide. "I know my shit."

"But what's up with the other dog?"

I take a few slow steps toward the Revenant. "It's not a dog." I kneel and hold my hand out. "It's a wolf boy."

The Revenant opens its red maw and lunges forward. I feel the warm jaws clamp onto my hand as Shannon screams and my eyes fill with dusk.

———

I OPEN MY EYES and I see it is one thirty in the morning on my computer screen. It has been hours since I began reading through pages and pages of tribal court documents, trying to piece together a solid case against Levi Dotson, the most crooked member of the tribal council.

There is a knock on the door. Years ago, I might have been afraid of such a thing but at thirty years old, I don't scare easily. Plus, I know this reservation like the back of my hand. There are plenty of unattractive and insidious parts of the land, but so far, I have survived three decades of it.

Outside the door, leaning against the wooden railing is a teenage boy. He is wearing a dark hoodie and baggy jeans, and half of his face is hidden. The other half is distressed, sobbing, in pain.

"Are you okay?" The boy shakes his head. "Are you hurt?" He nods his head up and down hard. The boy's arms are tight around his midsection, as if he's trying to hold himself together on trembling legs. "Come in. I'll get some help."

The boy staggers inside and collapses on the kitchen floor.

"Just stay strong. I'm going to call for help . . ."

"You don't need to call," the boy says. His voice is low and breathy, like he hasn't slept in days.

"What?"

"Please don't call anyone."

The computer monitor fades away into a dark screen saver and the only light that remains appears dimmer than just moments before. "I have to do something. You're bleeding!"

I didn't notice it when he was standing out in the dark, but on my bright linoleum floor the blood soaking through the hoodie is evident. "Don't worry. I don't have much left anyway. Most of it drained on the way here."

That can't be true. Otherwise the boy wouldn't still be moving. "You still have time! I just need to call . . ."

The boy wheezes out a laugh. "No more time."

I try to place a call but the phone is stuck on the lock screen. "Work, you piece of crap!"

"It won't." The boy climbs to his feet and staggers over to the couch. "No more time."

Time. I look at the screen's clock display and see it is not counting up. The setting was supposed to show the count of seconds and milliseconds, but it has stopped at 01:31:33.333.

"I told you, no more time. No more time—" The boy's voice breaks on the final word. "No more ... Can I ask you a favor before I die?"

"Of course, anything."

"Tell me about your daughter. And her mother. Please?"

"Maya?" I say. My head throbs. Something is wrong. This is not my voice. "She's great. She just turned thirteen. They say the teenage years are the hardest."

The boy laughs. "Yeah, I'll bet. I didn't make it out of them."

"I'm sorry."

"Don't be sorry. Be happy. I wanted to be but it's too late. Does Maya love you?"

"Yes. She tells me every night before she goes to bed."

"And Maya's mother?"

"We haven't been together for a while. But we spend every birthday and holiday together. My family and hers."

"So, you have a different girlfriend?"

"I have a wife. And twin boys. They were just born last year."

The boy lets out a pained howl and weeps thin, red tears. "So, you're pretty happy, aren't you? This life, do you think it's been good?"

I know it's not my voice that replies. "Yes. It's been a great life."

"I can't feel my body anymore. I can't taste the blood on my tongue or smell it on my clothes. But I can hear you. Please, hurry and tell me more."

I sputter out a collection of rambling sentences about my life with Maya, and my new wife, Patricia, the new boys, and my ex-wife, Gertrude. By the time I have nothing more to say, there are tears running down my eyes and I am shaking. The boy unzips his sweater, revealing a white-and-red basketball jersey soaked in blood. He removes it and there are multiple wounds on his body. "That fucker. He got me eight times and then he just left me there. Ran away like a little bitch. I can't believe she had to see me like that."

"I really should call someone, kid. I can save you. I want to help you."

The boy stares into my eyes. His are filled with red. "Not me. Help my daughter. Help her mother. Tell them I'm sorry. Will you do that?"

"I promise."

He stands up and walks out the door. Before he leaves he turns back. "What was the best moment in your life?"

The tears burn through my face as they fall. "When I held a baby for the first time." The picture burns bright in my mind. A young Native boy, no more than four, holding an infant boy in his hands. "This is Marion," a motherly voice whispers on the wind.

The bloodstained young man wipes his face and laughs. "Figures. I used to think it was when we won the state basketball championship. We were celebrating again tonight. Bad idea."

"Wait. Where—where exactly are you going?"

"Going to the Gizhay Manido Chapel. Come see me. I could teach you a lot, Marion."

As soon as the door shuts behind him, I fall to the floor. My body convulses and burns. I don't know who I am. But I know I don't belong here. I know I am not him.

THE DAYLIGHT COMES BACK and I feel my body collapse. In the distance in front of me, a dog is running away. At first I hear the rustling of the leaves under its paws but suddenly they stop, and I know I will not see the Revenant again.

I look up at Shannon. "What happened?"

"Dude, you let that mongrel lick your hand and then you fainted. What the fuck is wrong with you? I had to shoo it away because you were just sitting there!"

Basil wakes and runs to me. He rolls onto his back next to me and starts to lick my face. He is whining and panting. I've never felt so missed before. I pet him a few times and hold him until he is calm, and then I stand up to face Shannon, who looms over me like a Paul Bunyan statue.

"Total disclosure, I have no idea how to explain any of this." I lean into him and rest my body against his bulky frame. The smell of cigarettes and lake water fills my nostrils from his flannel. "I wish you had told me you were dating women again."

He wraps his hands around me and squeezes my back with his big hands, just a little too rough but just how I like him to do it. "I can't, Marion. I can't."

The tight embrace ends and he leaves. I watch him walk all the way up the trail, away from me and my sore back and hurting heart, and the engine of his truck is loud and booming as he starts it up and drives away.

Basil sits in front of me, tail wagging like crazy, and waits for me to pet him again.

"Come on, boy. Let's go for a walk."

It's five miles back to Geshig. By the time we get into town and find a ride home, we'll both need lots of sleep.

Ten

This Town Sleeps

THERE'S A TRUTH ABOUT this town that many live but few will ever admit: Geshig is the weight that crushes any form of ambition. *The sky is the limit* takes on a new meaning when it comes to motivating children. By the time children reach middle school, they know there is nothing for them beyond the highway.

Small towns don't feel timeless for a love of simpler times; their time and purpose in this world left long ago. For Geshig, the timelessness first started when the last lumber boom busted and the only thing worth a damn in the town was shipped away by train and used to make furniture across the Midwest. There are small pieces of Geshig's worth scattered throughout Fargo, Minneapolis, Des Moines, and Chicago. But not every tree was claimed.

The red pines pine for red-clad men to spare them from the eventless life of this town. Even a stationary object cannot stand the lethargy of Geshig.

When teenagers make their grandiose plans of leaving, they

say *There's nothing to do here.* They don't realize there are plenty of houses to burn down, railroad links to dig up, and roads to dismantle until the sun can once again shine on a patch of dirt thought lost to history. There is plenty to do in Geshig if the aim is to destroy Geshig.

Jeanie with the Long John Stare

SMALL TOWNS KEEP SACRED a silent watcher. Usually it's some folksy project designed to stroke the egos of its citizens who can boast of few things proudly. These towns are the same at the roots: bootstrap-strong and timeless, census growth nonexistent, always shrinking in people despite the declarations of love and pride from the citizens.

The sacred silent watcher can be a statue made by drunken lumberjacks or a simple wall erected around the community garden with handprints frozen in concrete. The watcher houses the spirit of the town. Not a ghostly spirit, but the idea of one place in time that declares itself important. A meaningless object that reassures the citizens: *It's here, therefore we are.*

The Geshig Elementary School takes a field trip every fall, and this one is half literal. In single-file lines that eventually morph into a group, the children are led from the back door of the school, past the playground, across a small field of grass, past the rusty merry-go-round, and to Jack's Lumberjack Shack, a museum sustained by field trip revenue.

Jeanie walks alone with downcast eyes. Only in fourth grade and already branded the weird girl by classmates. No friends yet, and maybe not ever, she fears. She walks into the lobby of the museum last and hates every moment.

The year of Jeanie's field trip doesn't matter. Jeanie could be a grandmother by now. Or she could have died young, buried behind the Episcopalian church. Likewise, the year that the log cabins behind the lumberjack museum were built doesn't truly matter. They look authentic enough to anyone born well after Geshig's last great lumber boom. No one is going to grade the authenticity.

Still, it does bring disappointment to some when they learn the dusty old wooden shacks were actually built in the late sixties by Jack Kressenbach, who worked in one of the last lumber camps when he was a boy. These sacred relics have been here for only half of Geshig's life.

The knowledge does not disappoint Jeanie because by now everything about school has disappointed her. She only gives the tour guide her attention because it's something new to the typical day and she does not have to feel singled out since none of the children are allowed to talk.

The guide leads them into the first cabin. Though just revealed as replicas, there is an authentic feel to them in the eyes of Jeanie and all the children. Every inch is covered in dust, or rather a dustlike coating has been layered over the wax fruit, wooden furniture, and clothes.

Hanging on a clothesline above the woodstove is a pair of pale, dirty long johns. The kind with the jockey lines and small checkered pattern, but with a hooked end for the feet, like a child's pajamas. Jeanie looked at the dirty pair of undergarments and felt a strange excitement and embarrassment.

Her face flushed and she ducked her head into her neck and shoulders. She wondered why none of the other kids were as embarrassed to see a man's underclothes just hanging above for all the world to see. There was something not right here, something moving.

Through the rest of the tour, Jeanie kept her head low and tried to focus but couldn't take her mind off those long johns. Were the dark stains real? What did the cloth feel like? What did they smell like? Each time the questions raced in her mind, she felt shame rush across her face again, but had an urge to giggle.

When she arrived home, she had an idea. A compulsion, really. She went to the laundry room in the basement and began to search through the dirty hamper. Inside she found socks, shirts, pants, her mother's panties, her brother's boxer shorts, her father's briefs, and one pair of pale gray long johns, also her father's.

She held them up to the basement light but didn't know what she was supposed to do. They were her father's so it felt wrong, but she wanted to take a whiff. She held them in front of her until she heard footsteps pound down the basement stairs.

"What the heck are you doing?" her older sister asked.

Jeanie dropped the pair back into the basket. "I'm trying to do laundry. I don't have any clothes for tomorrow."

Her older sister began to laugh. "You sure? You looked like you were playing with Dad's long underwear."

"Ick, not even!" Jeanie shouted. "I thought they were my pajamas."

"Mmmhmm. Sure, little sis." Her older sister laughed. "Just make sure to fold my stuff when you're done."

Immediately after getting caught, Jeanie ran into her room and hid under her covers. Scared that her sister somehow knew what she was doing. But slightly regretful that she hadn't brought the pair with her.

The fear of getting caught prevented her from exploring her newfound passion for months, until her mother surprised her at the beginning of summer with a trip to a local Bible camp.

Jeanie was not particularly fascinated with the idea of a religious summer camp, but it would be better than sitting at home bored until school started again. And perhaps in a different setting she could make some new friends.

The first night, when the other girls in the cabin were putting on their pajamas, she had another burst of inspiration and since none of these other girls were in her school, she would have nothing to lose if they laughed at her.

"We should sneak into the boys' cabin," she announced just before lights out.

"Why?" one of the other girls asked.

"I've seen it on movies. The boys are gonna try and steal our underwear," Jeanie said, holding back a smile. "We should do it to them first."

Not a single girl joined her, but for the first time Jeanie did not feel uncomfortable with the stares of other children. Before, she was Jeanie the Weird Girl and the eyes were mean, but now she was looked on in admiration. Her cabinmates watched her step out into the night like a heroine taking flight.

Not fifty feet away from the cabin, Jeanie was caught by a young camp counselor, whose name she never learned, but whose face she would remember for a long time.

"Whoa there, little camper," he said, while scooping her into his arms. "It's past your bedtime."

Jeanie said nothing as he walked her back to the cabin. She stared into his patchy scruff, his smile, and the red flannel arms that held her, and suddenly the long johns weren't important.

As she got back into her bunk, her mind raced with thoughts of a man in red, carrying her home from the dark of the woods.

A Sandman in the Shadows

IF YOU LIVE IN this town, you've seen him.

He is the nightmare of the hyperactive mind that cannot stop imagining the worst, and waking does nothing to stop it. He will find those in Geshig with dreams, if he were a spider and the web, the town.

On a normal evening, a young woman, black hair, bronze skin, beautiful beyond this town's beliefs, walks home. She has just finished an average shift at the Misi-Ziibi Pizzeria and is walking home from Main Street toward the east end. She is an ambitious woman, a dreamer who is saving up her waitressing tips to move to Fargo and attend NDSU. She will be a Bison, take courses, and play rugby.

The first step is making it home.

As soon as she passes the openness of the town's only busy section, trees become shrouds in every yard and the robin's-egg-blue evening sky becomes a smoky dusk from the foliage.

That's when he lays the trap.

"Hey, do you have a cigarette?"

The voice comes from behind her, and the young woman casually turns and smiles as if nothing is wrong. There are no strangers in Geshig. Except him. No one truly knows who he is. "I'm sorry, I . . . don't." As soon as the young woman sees the figure, her mood turns into the fear that all women have experienced.

The man she sees is wearing a long brown trench coat, appropriate for autumn weather, but not exactly a popular style around town. He also wears a gray plaid beret and has his hands in his coat pockets.

"Thanks anyway, miss."

The man does not murder or rape her. The man does not steal her money. The man does nothing but walk by and pat her on the shoulder. She is too frightened to pull away and prevent him from making contact, though she wanted to.

The fear that prevented her from pulling away is her undoing. She meets a fate worse than death for people with ambition.

She is sentenced to life in Geshig. She will never make the connection, but he has taken her ambition. He has sucked it from her heart like a ring of smoke looping back into a mouth and into tar-coated lungs.

Elsewhere in town, on another night, another year perhaps, a young and virile man is anxious for relief. He needs to empty himself in or on someone, and the first man who agrees gets into his car with no hesitation.

The riled-up man brings the other to a trail at a desolate end of town. They fuck. They do not make love, or hook up, service, mess around, or cuddle. They fuck until they are both satisfied. One is emptied and he is filled.

The man has sapped another resident of ambition, and the satisfied young man will never know why he cannot leave this silent town.

The Painted Silo

SOME SACRED SILENT GUARDIANS are true relics of the past, not replicas. The true guardian of Geshig has been romanticized only by paint. It stands higher than the replica log cabins nearby, and unlike the falseness of Jack's Lumberjack Shack, Geshig's guardian once had a true purpose. Octagonal in shape and painted on the bottom of each panel, there is a wooden silo in between two fenced gardens.

The images are in bright colors. One depicts an eagle holding a rose over the world and the Americas are visible. To the left is an Ojibwe medicine wheel with an eagle head and feathers hanging below. Farther left, the artist has painted a lynx or a fox, and a large pink lady's slipper. Another image depicts two traditional Ojibwe dancers. One is a shawl dancer with a feather in her hair. The other is a male fancy dancer who appears to be riding an eagle totem. In the very center of the silo's boarded-up door is one large and lone feather with one small medicine wheel on either side of it, like an Indian phallus in disguise.

The paint is chipping and fading away, as is the rest of the structure. Windows nailed shut and painted over are on three sides and a fourth has a door that has been boarded shut.

The silo was where the community would store wild rice during ricing season. *Manoomin* is the Ojibwe word for it. Traditionally told, the Ojibwe's presence in the Great Lakes area was because a vision of seven spiritual beings told them to follow where food grows on water. Just as the Ojibwe have fallen out of their traditional lifestyle, in the late seventies the silo fell into disrepair and became a blight on the community. In the mid-nineties there was a renewed interest in the relic and it was redecorated.

On either side of the silo is a garden. One is full of vegetables, lettuce, corn, tomatoes, and peppers. The garden on the other side appears to have fallen into obscurity. An aerial view of it shows a circular pattern of lines on a mound that could be a compass or a turtle's shell. Inside the garden only grass and weeds grow. No garden is perfect. No sacred guardian is perfect. The guardian, were it sentient, wouldn't want its secret revealed. Whether it's a sacred rock from outer space, the body of a missing child, a trove of silver and gold, or just a damp, moldy space where spiders, insects, and salamanders hold dominion, no one in Geshig will ever know until the structure is crushed by a felled tree during a summer storm or by a bulldozer when the land is turned into a development project for another unneeded building. No one will truly know.

Unless, of course, the secret of the sacred silent silo after so many years of neglect was awakened by the sound of a rusty merry-go-round, and brought new life to this sleeping town.

Eleven

White People's Ghosts

HEY SEXY LITTLE BOY. *I wanna scoop you in my arms and carry you to bed. ;)*

The man on the screen calls himself TractorMan. I decide to ignore the cringe-worthy comment and give him a chance.

At forty, he is fourteen years older than me but age has not mattered to me in a long time. As usual for older men, he is married—to a woman—and wants to revisit an old passion.

Haven't had it in so long, cutie, he writes.

Oh? How long?

Years. ;) You got a place we can do it?

I can host. I live in Half Lake.

Too far. I can't drive there. :(:(

That should be the end of it. But Shannon has not messaged me for over a week. I have a feeling this time he is gone for good. And right now, it seems my hands work faster than my head.

I know a place in Geshig. If you don't mind doing it in a car.

I prefer it!! ;) Love fucking boys in my truck.

Yet another warning sign. In theory.

I drive to a field in the south of Geshig right as the clock strikes two a.m. The leaves have already fallen, but the mix of the darkling night and densely packed trees shows nothing to anyone who might pass by. The trail is easy to miss from the road but I know this neighborhood better than any part of town.

Near the end of the trail, there is a small clearing that stops just before a steep drop and then the cold, gray shores of Lake Anders. Already parked is a big silver pickup and a dark figure, presumably my suitor and/or murderer.

When I get into the passenger seat, the overhead lights show me that he does look like the photo on his profile. Handsome, in a farmer kind of way. Black goatee and mustache littered with silver strands, beady eyes with crow's-feet, and once he finally takes his hat off, hair thinning just above the temples.

TractorMan's kiss is at first sloppy but slows down as he works his hands down my body.

He is taller and heavier than me, so my body is aching and possibly bruised when he stops riding me. We catch our breath for a few minutes and then he asks if I would like to join him in the bed of his truck.

"Sure?"

There are a few thick blankets in the bed that we lie on top of while we look at the late-autumn sky.

"How did you know about this place?" His breath tickles the back of my neck when he asks.

"I grew up like a mile from here. My house is still over there but we moved."

"Did you know no one would be here?"

"No. But no one ever was before."

"Let's do this again. Here. Same time."

"I really don't mind you coming over. Don't have to worry about anyone finding us. I mean, I'm not worried, but ya know, just in case."

"No." He pulls me tighter and breathes into my ear. "People know me in Half Lake. I can't risk being seen."

I hold in my laughter. Another man in my life afraid of being seen. It's my curse. I used to joke that it was a curse, but now that I've brought a dog back to life I'm more inclined to believe in those kinds of things.

My first boyfriend, Gordon, was an older guy, just like TractorMan, but nothing held him back. He had all the confidence needed to walk in the world with another man's hand in his and not care who saw. But it wasn't my hand. I dated him for half a year, told no one about him, not even my mother, and eventually we broke up because of that. I didn't want to but I did nothing to stop it from happening.

Now the only men who seem to want me are shadow men who can barely fuck with their eyes open.

Even though the night wind is cold on my exposed skin, I fall asleep wrapped in TractorMan's arms, feeling his warm breath on my neck. There are no images in the dream, just the feeling of a man holding me. But it's not the one in the truck. It's Shannon. The only man I want, and he's not even one of the four men I've slept with since he left me at the cabin.

TractorMan's body shudders and we both wake up. "Fuck, what time is it?" He checks his phone and his mouth puffs out a sigh of relief. "I guess we should go."

I leave the clearing without making any definitive plans with

TractorMan. At home, I check the app. His profile has disappeared from the grid. I'm relieved, because I'm sick of finding older men who say they're tops and then either deliver a poor, soft showing or prefer the bottom side of gay life. Good riddance, TractorMan, and good luck with your wife.

———

THE PHONE VIBRATES. A dead boy texts. Do you respond?

In the middle of the night, I wake to a text from the number 000-000-0000 that reads *Marion. Come to the chapel.*

When I wake in the morning the message is gone.

"Fine," I groan. In the bed next to me, Basil wakes, wags his tail, and puts his front paw right in my face. I cringe as his nails scrape just beneath my eyes. I need to get them trimmed.

"Do you wanna come with or no?" Basil jumps out of bed, circles around to my side, and taps his feet on the floor. Hunger. "Nah, probably not. Dogs are sacred or something. You better stay here, boy."

The first companion to the Original Man of Ojibwe myth was a dog. Somehow that makes dogs too sacred to be at things like powwows, so I assume it's the same for a half-Indian church.

I lay down a few of the pads I used to train him as a pup last summer and fill up his food and water dishes. I turn on the TV to some innocuous PBS show to keep some noise and images for him to focus on if he gets lonely, and then I leave.

The morning is dusted with encroaching November frost and my car takes about ten minutes to warm up and clear off. While I wait I pointlessly look at my texts and apps again for messages from him. He's by now made it clear he doesn't want to talk, and I've had the self-control for once to not blow up his phone, but the urge hasn't gone away.

The Gizhay Manido Chapel is named after the Ojibwe phrase for the Christian God, *gizhe-manidoo*, instead of *Gichi-Manidoo*, the original Creator (or Creatrix) of our lore. When the white people arrived I assume whoever came up with *gizhe-manidoo* wanted to differentiate their version of God with an equivalent phrase. If I'm not mistaken it means kind or loving God, which is kind of ironic considering what the priests did to Ojibwe people.

The chapel happens to be just a block from the elementary school park where all this nonsense started. It's a Saturday so the door is probably locked and I'm wasting my time. Still, I walk up to the front door, grab the faded gold handle, and turn.

Locked.

"Ah don't make me break in, Kayden." Luckily no one is around to see the exact moment I start to lose my mind. "Meet me halfway, here."

Right after I say the words, the handle clicks and turns on its own. The door opens slowly, and at the end of the sanctuary I see a lit candle. "Thanks," I say as I walk down between the pews. They are varnished with a wood-burned pattern of a simple leaf. Each armrest has an animal head carved into the end, and the entire vibe of the place feels like new-agey Indian ideas. A beaded floral blanket is spread above the front of the church with a large wooden crucifix hanging in the middle.

"So, I'm here," I say when I reach the front of the room. "Where are you?"

The candle blows out, the door shuts, and in the corner of my eye I see a figure moving.

He is sitting in the front row of the pews and stands up with a heave and a sigh, as if tired and discontent with the meeting. The ghost of Kayden Kelliher walks up to me and stands mere inches away. He holds out his hand to shake but I don't move.

"Thinking about what Carey said?" he asks. His voice is deep and flowing with the elongated sounds of the rez accent.

"Yeah. Not to trust ghosts."

The ghost of Kayden Kelliher laughs. "Yeah, what did he call them? White people shit?"

"Yeah."

"Ignore him. He's just a human. Doesn't know shit about shit. Grab a seat, let's talk."

Kayden sits down in the front row again and stares at the cross on the wall. I join him but keep my distance. "So how does this work? I get three questions, vague answers, and then you steal my spirit?"

"What spirit? You don't believe in this."

"Let's say for now I do."

"Then ask away. We have nothing but time." Kayden laughs. "A dwarf spirit told me that time is all time. Do you know what that means?"

"Sounds like dime-store philosophy."

"Nah. I think he meant time is a false idea, that there is only the present."

"What do you think of that?"

"I'd love for it to be true if it meant I didn't die twelve years ago."

"Fair enough. So, I guess my first question would be, was that you inside the dead dog? Did you possess it or something?"

"Oh boy, here we go. How to explain. It wasn't—" He puts his hand over his chest. "Me. The form you're seeing now. It was a part of me."

"And that part, it's been with me for years? Because of my mother's kiss?"

"Ha. Good guess. But no, that's not quite it." Kayden stands up and walks to the table. Instead of reaching through solid objects like in movies, he's able to pick up what looks like an Ojibwe songbook with a beaded leather cover. "I've been clinging to your life ever since the moment I died, Marion."

"Why me?"

"Because I wanted to think about my baby. Maya … her name is Maya, right?"

"You don't know?"

"Not this part of me. I can't choose where I go, Marion. You ever see a pitch-black night with no stars? That's kind of what it's like to be me now, only I'm behind the sky. I see a flicker of light and I follow it, but I never stay for long." Kayden shrugs his ghostly shoulders. "I can't watch over her."

"I'm sorry."

"It's okay. I don't feel a lot of sadness anymore. Just a longing to reach life again." He takes a step toward me. "Don't worry. I'm not trying to steal your life. I could, but I'd have done that years ago if I thought I'd enjoy the things you like, no offense."

"None taken. I just hope you've enjoyed the view."

"Can't say I haven't laughed a time or two … you fucking my old basketball coach, that was a bit of a shock."

I don't even know who he's talking about, but I don't doubt him.

"So why did you bring Basil to the red pine cabin?"

"How long has it been since a cabin was there? Since any of your family actually lived there?"

"I think it was torn down in like '86?"

"I can't imagine life without my family, yet here I am, without my family. My life story is the people I left behind. Including you." He puts his hand on my shoulder. It feels just as real and tangible as if he was alive. "We are brothers, Marion. Before all this, we were. Because I held you. Do you know what the last thing that went through my mind was when I was alive? Not my mother. Not my grandfather. Not my beautiful Gertrude. Not the baby we made growing inside of her. It was you, Marion.

"When your mother brought you back to our house after you were born, I held you. The first and only baby I ever got to hold." A silvery tear falls from his spirit eyes and drifts away before it hits the floor. "Now I feel sadness … I'm afraid I've held you back. Because I couldn't handle leaving, I kept bringing you back here. But I think there's something you could do to help me leave."

"What's that?"

Kayden Kelliher leans forward and a pair of wispy lips touches my forehead. "Let her meet her father."

"Kayden … I'm sorry. I can't do that. I love Maya too, but that is way too personal … And honestly, I don't trust you. Whatever you are, wherever you came from, I don't know what it is and I won't be responsible for bringing that on her if this is some trick."

He stares into my eyes and his start to glow with sparkling silver lights. A pointy-toothed smile spreads across his face. "If you do, maybe I'll tell Gordon to visit you."

I stand up right away but he is drifting away from me. His

legs are moving as if he is walking, but his frame drifts along faster than his legs move, like the red rug has become an airport walkway. I run after him.

"Kayden? Kayden!"

He disappears into the door, and right as I shout the door opens.

Gerly and Maya walk in, hand in hand. They both stare at me with narrowed eyes. "What did you say?"

"Oh ... Hello. What are you doing here?"

"I clean up here on Saturdays. What are *you* doing here?" Gerly asks. "And why did you shout 'Kayden'?"

I have no ideas on how to explain this, so I decide honesty is the best policy.

"About that ... Can I have a talk with you? Maybe without Maya."

Gerly takes a breath, holds silent, and then nods. "Baby girl, will you go play at the park for a bit? Thanks, sweetie."

Maya turns back to the front door, not taking her questioning eyes off me for a moment until the door shuts behind her.

"So, there's more than one Kayden in the world," Gerly says. "But I think I know which one you're talking about."

I sit down on the opposite side of the church this time, same row. "Ah, goddamn, where to begin ..."

"In a church, boy."

"Sorry."

I start from the beginning, and unlike with Shannon I don't preface it with any *you're not gonna believe me*s or doubts about my sanity. I tell her what happened from the moment I resurrected the dog from the merry-go-round. The graveyard. The dog showing up at my mother's house two hours away from here. The sweat lodge and the visit to the red pine cabin lot. But I leave out whatever happened there and what I saw, only that he told me to visit him here.

She is pale-faced when I finish but the color quickly returns when she starts to talk. "So, what are you thinking about all this?"

"Do you want my full truth?"

"Always."

"I'm wondering why it doesn't seem like you're grieving for him. Why it feels like the town has just—forgotten him."

She purses her lips and folds her hands in her lap. "Now it's my turn for a long story. If you need to piss, get up and go now."

"I'm fine."

"Okay. I'm going to tell you about Kayden Kelliher."

Twelve

Two Sisters

Brotherhood

THEY CALL US TRIBE. Band. Clan. When times were tough, our
tribes banded together, no matter what clan. When we needed
food and shelter we shared. When they fought us, we fought
back. When we needed protection, we protected each other.

Now they call us gangs. But these are not our words.

My father valued brotherhood above all else. When he talked
about his navy career, he always swore about the leaders and the
organization itself. But not his brothers. "I miss the brotherhood.
There was nothing like it," he'd say once he drank enough beers.

"I want a brother," I told him.

"Your mother can't have more babies."

"Why?"

"Her belly hurts too much. It won't work."

"Then can I have a baby? He can be my brother."

My father's smile was always lopsided when he was drunk.
It wasn't a happy look. It was a sad, desperate smile that spoke to

his longing. "No. You can't have any babies. You're gonna stay my little girl forever. My little Gerly."

He was right. After that, I was always Gerly to him. Even when he called from prison and I refused to talk to him, my mother would tell me that my father was asking for his Gerly.

Two Sisters

MY PARENTS TRIED TO explain to me over and over how the baby in the other woman's stomach was my brother or sister but I would not understand. My grandmother said it was because my eyes were too "green with envy" that I couldn't get it. I tried to tell her that she was wrong, that I really wanted a baby brother or sister but she didn't hear me any more than I heard my parents.

Angela, my Angie, she was born one month after my fifth birthday to a gestational surrogate. She was a plump baby and stayed that way into her child- and adulthood. I proved my grandmother wrong by loving her as soon as she was brought home. I did not fully understand the specifics of her birth until years later, but I never cared.

"She looks like me," I told my mother over and over when I first held her in my arms.

"That's because you look like me," she said, taking her back from me. I was only allowed to hold her for a few moments at a time.

Later when we were alone, my father asked me if I was okay with a little sister instead of a little brother. I told him yes, because she was so cute and looked like me. I don't think I was disappointed at all. "Good. Because we won't be able to give you a brother."

If he hadn't been secretly disappointed about that, maybe he wouldn't have missed out on raising his second daughter. Maybe he wouldn't have sought out that brotherhood that he craved. Maybe he wouldn't have robbed a casino with his gang and got caught. You know about that, right?

That was my father. But he's nothing to me now but a robber. And a murderer.

Defense

I WAS TWELVE YEARS old when I saw big, tough Kayden Kelliher cry.

Back then I was one of the competitive kids in gym class. My favorite was floor hockey but whatever game we played I gave it my all. I think it was because of my name. Before my father went to prison I liked it because I hated my full name. By the time I got to middle school and he was locked up, I despised both. Who wants to be called girlie? No one. Not girls or boys.

Every time I heard it, I was motivated to not be what it implied. I never wore skirts or bright colors. Never fixed my hair. It was basketball shorts and jerseys for me.

The game was close. My team was only one point behind, and because our junior varsity team's best player was on the other, that was a big deal. I was more determined than ever to win, and we both played hard.

Kayden towered over me and his arms waved out far and

wide, but I was faster and more agile. Like he danced shawl and I was the grass dancer. Near the end of the court I dropped the ball and he dove for it. I was close behind him and ready to try to block when I saw his hand reach behind him toward me. Before I could react, his hand was on my chest.

I froze, stared at him, and then ran out of the gym. In the counselor's office, I told her about what had happened, or what I thought had happened, with tears in my eyes. She listened to every word and wrote up a harassment report on Kayden.

Later there was a meeting between me, the counselor, the principal, and Kayden. He was asked to explain why he had groped me. He broke down crying, saying it was just an accident because we were playing basketball and both of us were trying hard to win. The adults didn't let me tell my side of it. After he spoke, they asked me if what he said made sense, if I was sure that he did it on purpose, if I wasn't just imagining something wrong.

I told them yes and accepted his apology. The report was thrown out and no action was taken. Me and Kayden did not talk about it until five years later, on the first night we made love. When we created our little girl together.

Just two months later, my daughter's father was stolen from us.

Clash

THERE WERE NO ADULTS around when Kayden and Jared fought for the first time. It was the fall of our sophomore year and we'd just started dating. I hadn't even kissed him yet. The most

I was willing to do with him was hold his hand as we walked through the hallways.

One morning in school, he seemed agitated during breakfast. He told me he didn't get enough sleep because he was up late thinking about me. But it wasn't like him to stay up late, nor was he easily bothered. I didn't press him on the subject, and when he told me he needed to go "take care of something," I was immediately suspicious.

I watched him walk toward the D wing of the school. It was a wing with few classrooms or teachers because of budget cuts over the past few years of poor test scores. Somehow this area wasn't much noticed by the staff.

I didn't follow Kayden down the wing. It would've been too obvious. Instead I walked around the other three wings in a big loop until I found where he and a group of three other boys were. I could hear them around the corner discussing something that sounded serious.

"He doesn't care who your grandfather is." It was Jared Haltstorm's voice I heard. "He wants your family to know they're marked now."

"Marked? What's that supposed to mean?" That was Kayden.

"It means we're gonna take you all the fuck out, that's what."

"Don't even fucking go there, Jared. Some things you just don't play around with."

"Like *arson*?"

"Arson? Why the fuck are you bringing up arson?"

"Because Levi knows it was your bitch-ass that did it. He knew how much product was in there and you burned that shit up. You killed him. You're gonna get yours for that."

"If you wanna keep talking, little boy, keep doing it. Don't you fuckin' dare accuse me of shit I didn't do."

The sounds went from voices to hard hits and angry grunts. I peered around the corner and saw Kayden and Jared were on the ground, each trying to land punches. I watched for a few moments, not really sure why, but then I ran. The smart thing would have been to run for an adult but instead I went to my locker, grabbed my books, and walked to class.

Later, after his suspension, Kayden told me that a teacher happened to walk by and radioed for the school officer to break it apart. But he wouldn't tell me who won the fight, or if whatever problems they had were resolved. What he did tell me was that Jared was mad at him because he thought he was trying to steal his girlfriend.

I never told Kayden I knew he had lied right to my face.

Odaanisan (His Daughter)

IN A HOTEL IN Minneapolis, where the whole school was staying for the state championship, Kayden and I planned our future. When the celebration had settled and Kayden had the championship medal around his neck, we made love the first time.

We knew before we started that we wanted a family. It was almost an unspoken decision, but after we finished and for the second time that night he was out of breath, he said, "I want an Ojibwe name."

"What?"

Then he smiled at me with those big wolfy teeth. "For our son."

"Nope," I said. "Our *sons*. And daughters. All four of them."

"Why four?"

"Why not?"

My question was answered less than two months later when I held him in my arms as he died.

Gii-shoomiingweni (He Smiled)

JARED WAS ASKED TO join the basketball team by a lot of people. His friends who had joined. Coaches. Even Kayden asked him about it in class, where both of them knew better than to bring up their issues. He would have brought height, something that their lineup usually lacked.

But the lack of Jared did not matter. Our team went all the way to state and won without him. I wonder sometimes if that made him jealous. Seeing a band of brothers unite and reach their goal instead of just lying around town and getting high. Maybe he would not have been a good player. Not every tall Indian has the talent or love for it. But the coaches would have tried to make a good player out of him, and even sitting on the bench throughout the season would have still given him a ribbon. A place. Respect.

At the party I was the only sober one. I knew I was pregnant with Maya, so Kayden would not let me drink. He did not drink for the first few hours either but as the night grew darker and the teammates became wilder, Kayden had no choice but to try to keep up.

Midnight was when his mood fell. I noticed he kept glancing at his phone as the hour passed and tried to ask him what was wrong. He said it was nothing but by then I knew what it sounded like when he was lying to me.

He asked me to go inside and get some swamp tea ready for him. His family drank it a lot and claimed it cured all kinds of things. I nodded and walked inside. Then, instead of walking into the kitchen and preparing his drink, I walked out the back door and hid behind his family's big white propane tank.

Kayden did not want tea. He wanted me distracted.

I watched him leave the fire and walk toward a thicket of woods behind his house. After there was a good distance between us, I followed him. I took off my shoes to quiet my steps. I held my hands over my stomach, over Maya, when I first heard Kayden's voice shout.

"Levi! Where the fuck are you? We're gonna finish this."

His first scream was worst. It was pain and shock. Jared later said he had caught Kayden by surprise and slashed him across the back. The rest of his screams came quieter until finally it sounded like he was throwing up. By the time I reached him, he was flat on the ground and Jared was running into the darkness. Just like me, Kayden was holding his stomach, convulsing, trying to breathe.

I remember that the sky was dark. There was no moon and the stars did not give much light. But still, I could see his face when I knelt to him. His eyes were scared but when he saw me, he smiled his wolf grin and grabbed my hand.

The Arsonist

I CALLED THE COPS with Kayden's cell phone. And then I hid it in my shirt. If you read the reports, you won't see it listed at the crime scene. It was found later in his bedroom, where I hid it after reading through and deleting his messages.

When I knew he was dead, I lost all control of my thoughts. I was screaming and crying and yet somehow I had managed to find his cell phone in his sweater, make the call, and then hide it.

I had had my suspicions about him for a while. Ever since the fight between him and Jared, I knew there were parts of his life that he did not tell me about but that was easy to ignore when he was holding my hand and treating me like a princess.

I don't know how I ended up at my grandmother's house but I woke up the next morning aching all over. My eyes, my head, my chest. My stomach. I held my stomach and prayed for hours. I was so scared that I was going to lose Maya that my body was shaking. I just knew it was going to happen any moment.

Kayden wanted children so badly. He had wanted to be a father for so long and he wasn't going to be. I called out his name over and over. When my voice was gone and my tears were dried, it was then I noticed that my stomach no longer hurt. I stopped worrying. I kept grieving but I stopped worrying.

When I could pull myself out of bed I took a shower and then finally opened the cell phone. Kayden wasn't stupid. Most of the gang members weren't but there was one who stupidly made his text signature ~NDN BLOODZ 4 LIFE!~. Even if it hadn't been there, I could read between the lines of the texts and see that Kayden was in the gang. The very last text he got was a warning from an unknown number that Levi Dotson was on his way to *kick your ass* for burning Lonnie's house. I could barely hold the phone.

That's what Kayden died for. Lonnie Barclay's meth house.

Did he burn it down? I don't know. I'll never know and I don't care, but regardless of if he did, it doesn't mean he deserved what happened. I struggled with that for a long time, Marion. Wondering how I could grieve for a man I loved who did things I despised. Things that took my father away from me. Kayden knew that, and he joined the gang anyway and hid it from me.

You know the rumors about the tribal council, right? Well, I can't confirm any of those, but I know two things happened in the year after Kayden's death. My mother, still married to my father, got an approval for a new house to be built. She'd only meant to request some funds for repairs, but the offices urged her to apply and they expedited it.

Then later that year, another woman got a house too. Brenda Haltstorm. She still lives there. I don't know her well, but Kayden's mom says she's doing better. Anyway, she lived in a bad trailer on the edge of town and also found herself approved for a building project. The tribal college kids built it, so the council basically paid themselves.

Odd, isn't it? The wife of a prisoner, a known gang leader, gets a free house, same as the mother of a murderer, a murderer who was in the same gang.

Now, I've got no proof of this or I would've come forward long ago. But I never visited my father after that. Maybe I will, but I ain't in a hurry for it. I know the day I do, the only thing I'm going to ask him is why, and no matter what he says, I'm gonna walk away no worse for wear. Because I've already been through the worst.

No, I don't grieve for Kayden every day. I don't grieve for him in the way I used to. I will miss Kayden every day of my life, and I see his face every time I look at Maya, but sometimes I can't even remember that part of my life easily. I only remember being pregnant and crying over a man who betrayed me by joining a gang, but who I loved with every part of my being, my spirit.

Thirteen

The Basketball Champion

WHEN GERLY FINISHES, SHE smiles and shrugs. "I don't know what's going on with you and Kayden, but if it's real ... you can understand, I don't want to be a part of it."

"Understand completely. I don't even want to be a part of it."

"That's life, kid. Look, I've already shed my tears for Kayden. Now and then I wake up after dreaming of him and maybe there's a small tear or two. I know I'll never be over it but I'm comfortable where I'm at with him. I don't need to revisit."

"Thank you for telling me all that, Gerly. I'm sorry you had to though." I laugh. "If all this is real, he probably planned this, so maybe it was inevitable."

"Spirits can be bitches like that."

She stands and walks to the front of the room. The crucifix hangs above like it's waiting for her. "So, your turn. Tell me about Gordon."

"It's stupid. Nowhere near as ... meaningful as your story."

"Tell it anyway, kid."

"Do you remember I used to live in Minneapolis?"

"Yeah."

"He's why I moved back to Geshig."

It started in my second year at a tech college. I was going for a general business degree, but didn't have a lot of passion for it. I was good at the accounting courses but even that late into the program I wasn't sure if it was what I really wanted.

There was a lot of want from me in those days. Pining for something more out of life. Then I discovered meeting men through the Internet, through phone apps, and I thought my calling had been found. I wasn't destined to be a businessman. I was destined to do business with men.

In my first semester of college, I met a man named Gordon through one of the apps. He was a bit older than me, thirty when I was still eighteen. He was my first boyfriend, but I left him the night after we first had sex because it freaked me out. I'd only been out to my mother, no one else, and being that sort of intimate with a man was a big step I wasn't ready to take.

Two years after I left him, I saw his obituary. Meth overdose. I had no one to tell this to, not my mother, not a friend in the world who would understand.

I couldn't be in the city that introduced me to him so I fled back home to Geshig. It's been five years and I'm still in this town.

Gerly listens to me silently and smiles when I finish. "I'm a lifer here. I got no reason to leave, and I don't want to. But you don't belong here. You don't even live in Geshig, but it seems like Half Lake ain't your town either, kid."

"I've wanted to leave for a while now."

She pats me on the shoulder. "You'll have to say goodbye to Maya first."

"You sure? Do you trust him?"

"Not entirely. But I'm not worried." Gerly walks to the altar and lights a branch of sage and sweetgrass in a cowrie shell. "I know she'll be safe."

———

OUTSIDE AT THE PARK, Gerly sits down on a bench. Maya runs over from the basketball court. Her breathing is quick, but she doesn't look tired out. She holds a faded black basketball between her forearm and her hip.

"Uncle Marion is out of practice," Gerly says. "You should show him how to play twenty-one."

"But he's taller than me!"

"Your dad wasn't that tall and he was the best."

"Okay. You ready, punk?" Maya says. Suddenly her voice isn't soft and cheery, but a commanding bite.

She quickly goes over her rules for twenty-one—Kayden's rules, which her older cousins taught her—and we begin.

I don't like basketball. Or most sports really, but something about basketball is particularly boring to the point of contempt. Maybe it's because I never played but went to a high school that revolved around it. Or maybe it's because I don't like fish tanks. I find nothing entertaining in staring at living things moving back and forth in an enclosed space.

But clearly I'm in the minority. I've seen enough enthusiasm on the rez to know that. Did you know you can just order a trophy from a company and engrave it however you want? I ordered myself a trophy in the exact size, shape, and fake plastic luster as the one state basketball championship trophy that sits in my high school's awards cabinet. Except instead of being about basketball, my trophy says *Marion Lafournier, World's Biggest Cynic.* And really, who could blame me?

A billboard in the middle of this town tells the children PLAY BALL, DON'T SMOKE METH.

As if basketball ever really saved any Indian from it. Near as I can tell, all it does is build up expectations and make the desire for mental escape even stronger when those expectations fail. A state championship near loss is still a loss. Tears are on the court. A small town puts on the face of pride, but everyone is filled with shame and regret. The star player enters adulthood at a loss for purpose, gets a job at the casino or tribal office, drinks, smokes, and breeds. Repeat.

A more accurate message on the billboard might be PLAY BALL, DEFINE YOUR LIFE BY YOUR LOVE OF IT, AND THEN TURN TO METH WHEN THE COLD, HARD FACTS OF LIFE SHATTER YOUR DREAMS.

Yes, I've earned that trophy. And Kayden earned his.

Kayden Kelliher spent years playing basketball. He trained his whole life for the championship and earned the first-place ribbon around his neck. And in the end, none of it mattered as he bled out in his backyard. Jared Haltstorm will only return to this town to be buried. Basketball did nothing to save either of them.

Maya scores the first point easily. I stumble around awkwardly, partially out of fear of tripping and falling into her small frame. After each point, the opposing team gets the shot, but they have to start at the half-court line and make the same shot as the previous one. Kind of like horse, but no penalties for missing, nor are there any breaks. The other team has to get the ball and defend quick as they can, no mercy. Eventually, there seem to be no rules at all.

And I miss. I miss every shot until Maya gets to ten points, basically halfway over with.

I am out of breath. I am hacking my weed-coated lungs out. I am . . .

The first point that is not Maya's is scored. The ball falls through the net with a crisp swish. It rebounds to the girl's hands and she sets the next play with a shot from the three-point line, and it just barely swirls into the rim.

The next shot leaves these hands from the same line and glides into the hoop, and again, and again. The two combatants circle around and around the half-court and soon they are neck and neck: twenty points to twenty points. And the final point goes to the girl after she narrowly misses a block by the boy who stares at her in fierce admiration.

"That's game," Maya says, turning back to the boy.

And then the basketball champion kisses his daughter on the forehead.

The black dots, the kind of fuzzy vision you get when standing up too fast, that's what happens to me when Kayden leaves. I can't see where he goes but I know he is no longer with me, and not with Maya, or with Gerly, who stares at us with tears in her eyes.

"That was . . . a good game," she says. "A damn good game."

I grab my stomach. "I need water. Or a stretcher."

Gerly grabs Maya's hand and they walk back to the church. I wave them off and take a short walk around the park to catch my breath.

On the far side, the merry-go-round is gone and left behind is a small patch of thin grass. No skeleton underneath, no dog, no Kayden.

Just a forgotten rumor.

Fourteen

Hey, Lumberjack

THE FIRST TIME YOU met the girl, it was while wearing a red flannel shirt, tight blue jeans, and an olive-green hat with a walleye with a hook in its mouth embroidered on the front. She walked right up to you at the bar and said, "Hey, lumberjack."

At first you thought she wasn't local. Most girls are used to the sight of guys like you, and rarely do they prance over so confidently and demand attention.

She called herself Jeanie, short for Jeanette, and from the first moment she spoke her eyes couldn't stop falling to your beard and below. Just like Marion. All he ever does is stare at your beard while rubbing your chest hair and waiting for another kiss.

So, you decided that this girl was the one. Right when she looked into your eyes and giggled at something dumb you said. That's when you knew it was right.

There was no waiting, no long courtship or dates. She fed you shots of tequila while she nursed a Guinness and eventually a tall glass called a Gets-Me-Naked was brought out with two straws. It tasted like a watermelon got fucked by acetone but it delivered what it promised.

Somehow, you two ended up back at her place. You don't remember the how but that wasn't important, only what happened next.

Kissing. Lots of it, and moans. Hers.

A belt unbuckled, a skirt unzipped, and then your face tickling her thighs as she held your head between her trembling hands.

Because you're a man's man. You're not some faggot who likes to kiss men with prickly beards or big muscles. You love pussy. You love women.

Marion would hate me if he knew.

That was all you could think about as you fucked her. Or she fucked you. The Gets-Me-Naked got right on top of you, so she took control while you laid back and waited for the big finish.

She got hers and you pretended you got yours, and then you passed out with your arms wrapped around her. She was either asleep or pretending to be when you whispered, "Marion," because the next day she didn't kick you out. The night did not end.

The girl who called you lumberjack keeps in contact with you, and these messages you don't erase right away. You keep them sacred instead of erasing them like his. Finally, a person you don't hide from. A body you don't feel disgusted by when you're done.

A person your family would be proud to know.

Hey, lumberjack, maybe you finally found a wife.

MARION HASN'T TEXTED SINCE the day down at the Quarry Way cemetery, but you don't care. You've moved on, he's moved on, it's over.

The girl is planning a dinner. She wants the meeting with the parents to go well, and it apparently involves switching between several cookbooks, setting the table just right, and keeping her apartment in top shape, not one knickknack or decorative pillow out of place.

She's a perfectionist, not like him.

His bedroom was a pigsty, and his house wasn't much better. It smelled like dog hair and shit, and a cheap attempt to cover it with a eucalyptus-oil diffuser that always made your nose feel funny when you woke up.

The girl knows how to keep a clean house. She knows how to cook, and most importantly, how to order you around. Table setting, measuring out food, pouring just the right amount of red wine and not a drop more. All things you do at her behest, and not in a commanding way.

Like a grandmother, she has a soft voice as she says, "Shannon, could you bring me the colander?" for her boiled potatoes, hand-peeled. The lines she traces on your shoulder when you complete the task, you could live for this. You'd give up everything to live for this.

The doorbell rings and the parents arrive, her mother and father.

They are everything you expect to have raised this angel from the bar. God-fearing and folksy, like a couple straight out of *Fargo*, almost like your own parents. The type who could raise a girl that drinks dark beers and hard liquor, rough and tumble in the streets, a picturesque woman in the kitchen. This is what it's all about.

Marion wouldn't know how to talk to this couple. He'd make it political, mention something about them living on stolen land or their white privilege or something else soapboxy. He's a stubborn man, but she's the perfect girl.

You pass the evening with flying colors, answer every question her father has about your job, your retirement plans, the type of truck you drive and the teams you root for, and you glow for the mother who has always wanted a son. She would be doting on you if the girl wasn't already doing that.

Hey, lumberjack, you've found the perfect family.

You don't even know anything about Marion's family.

—————

THE DOORBELL RINGS ON a day when your roommate isn't home and standing on the porch with a rolled-up towel in hand is a wiry, older Ojibwe woman with raspberry-chocolate hair and a smile like a romance novel ending. Something about her just screams gorgeous to you, as if you met your soul mate but thirty years too late.

"Shannon? You look so handsome." That novel smile has a secret, some kind of twist ending that you don't like.

"Do I know you, ma'am?"

"You used to come over when you were just a boy, so maybe. My name is Hazel. You and my son Marion used to be friends."

Life freezes for what feels like ten long, painful, torturous seconds. *Bezhig, niizh, niswi . . .*

"What did he tell you?" The words can barely squeeze through your clenched teeth.

"What world do you live in where Native boys talk to their mothers?" Her smile is coy, and you lose your temper.

"You got three seconds to tell me what you're doing here, lady, or I slam the door in your face."

"I know what he sees in you now." She laughs, a deep smoky kind of laughter. "If you're scared, we can take this inside. I would like to talk to you about something."

"That's not what I asked for."

"I can tell you why it's not working between you two. Why it may never work."

You feel the urge to fill with hot anger and scream at this bitch's face. Nothing ever needs to "work" because you don't do shit with guys, you're not a faggot. You're going to tell that to this woman's face and then shut the door.

"Okay . . . Come in."

In the living room, you bring her a cup of dark coffee and then pace around. How long until the roommate comes home? Is it an early day at work for him? What if he walks in, what do you say?

"Has my son told you anything about our family?"

"I don't remember."

"Probably not. Little brat likes to pretend we don't exist. He gets that from me though." She turns the bundled towel over in her hands. "Before I show you this, I just want to tell you a bit about my family."

As she tells the story, some of it comes back to you from when Marion talked about it on the way to the cemetery.

"I always thought it was just one of my aunt's ghost stories. They talked about it more than my mother did, but all of them were convinced it was real. I grew up afraid of being with any man because they talked about a curse so much, but eventually I grew out of that. And then, back into it. Marion's father went off to war, just like mine did. He came back, but he never once tried to speak to me again. Or meet his son. I believe this thing is why."

The towel comes unwrapped and in Hazel's lap is a glossy, black statue of a half ring of teeth.

"My grandmother Bullhead cut her husband's throat and then took out his jawbone. Then she used what she knew of her tribe's teachings to keep its spirit at bay, but she couldn't live forever…I suspect she wanted to spare her children from having to be attached to this thing so she had Tomas bury it with her ashes. But we are still dealing with it."

The jawbone is cold when she puts it in your hands, and rock solid.

"What do you want me to do with it?"

"I don't know. Burn sage in it. Break it. Use it as an ashtray. Whatever you want, but I've had a husband for years now, one spiritually strong enough to resist the kind of bad medicine this thing has on our family. But Marion isn't, so I fear that you're either in danger, or just your relationship is in danger." Hazel stands up and walks to the front door. "If you truly want to be with my son, I'm sure you'll figure it out." She leaves without another word.

Hey, lumberjack, if what she says is true you have two

choices. Leave well enough alone, and Marion will continue to leave you alone.

Or break it. Smash it to pieces. And prove to both him and his mother that this thing is just a fake. There's no curse, no bad medicine. Just paranoid Indian shit.

You take it outside, stand on the sidewalk, and slam it into the concrete like a football after a touchdown.

Under the sooty black layers white teeth shatter and spread across the road.

———

HEY, LUMBERJACK, YOU'RE GOING to come out one day.

You're going to go out fishing and say everything that you've never wanted to say.

To your father. His reaction is key. If it doesn't go well with him, your world will end and you will kill yourself.

To your mother. Her reaction will be easier, you think. She used to speak fondly of her gay friend in college, and she watches *Ellen* every day.

You wonder what will change. Family is one thing, work is another.

Hey, lumberjack, what's working worth if you're not happy with the life it's paying for?

———

THE PHONE RINGS TWICE before Marion answers.

"Hello?"

"Hey, babe," you say. It feels unnatural to say this to a man, yet it's exactly what feels right. There's a lightness in your chest as soon as the words come out, and you know now. It's him. "I miss you."

"Shannon ..."

"Just listen ..." Hey, lumberjack, it's now or never. *Bezhig, niizh, niswi* ... "I can't be the man you want overnight, Marion. But I will be one day. I'll be ready for you ... I think I love you, and I don't know if you'll understand this, but that isn't a good feeling right now. But I want it to be. I feel so wrong every day when I think about you, but I also feel more complete than I've ever felt. I don't know how to deal with this, but I know that I want to deal with it with you. If you'll let me."

"Shannon, I'm moving to Minneapolis."

Hey, lumberjack.

You waited too long.

Epilogue

Awake

SHANNON HAS AGREED TO buy my house. I've inspired him to finally get out of the town we grew up in and move away. Only, he's moving twenty miles and I'm moving two hundred. Again. Hopefully for the last time.

Basil will be staying here.

I love him, I really do, but he's a country dog. He loves walks in the woods and running through fallen leaves and chasing other animals. He loves Geshig, and because Shannon works there he'll be there a lot, even during work hours.

Maybe Basil is just like me. He was born in this town and even though something brought him away, he went back and enjoyed it. I could've enjoyed so much more about Geshig though.

Year-round events that I've taken for granted now seem like major attractions. In February, Lake Anders has an Eelpout Festival where men and women will get drunk, go ice fishing, and catch the ugly eelpouts that are the namesake of the reservation. Sometimes they'll even kiss them. In late spring, there's a 5K on the Tamarack Walk that pays out great prizes for the winners, not that I'd ever place, but I could've challenged myself.

There's a barbecue festival in the middle of summer when the sun is turning everyone's skin as red as the pots of chili for the annual cook-off. There's various powwows for the different holidays: Fourth of July, Labor Day, Memorial Day—and those are always good for fried food, maybe some hominy and wild rice soup.

But that's not the Geshig that I knew in the last few years of being here.

The day I move away, and Shannon and I exchange nothing but a handshake to transfer ownership of house and dog, I don't take the highway on the south end of Half Lake to get down to the cities. I take a detour home and visit the park one last time. It's still just a park.

I walk to the painted silo where I used to take part in the community garden in elementary school. The tradition is still carried on, but right now the plots are covered with the first blankets of November snow.

For just a moment, I consider walking back to the spot where the merry-go-round used to be. Ever since Kayden left, I have felt a strange incompleteness that I think will only be solved by finally leaving. I would stay if just one more time I could go to that merry-go-round and remember everything about why I came back, why I used to love it here.

But it's better to wake up than fall back asleep in a town with no dreams.

Acknowledgments

THE JOURNEY TO THIS novel passed through a lot of darkness, but I'm grateful for the people who fill my life with light and help bring out my best. This work couldn't have been possible without the ever-present love of my family, friends, and the organizations who took a chance on me and shared their wisdom.

To my agent, Eleanor, who believed in me and guided me through my first contract. To my editor, Harry, who helped me shape the book into its final form.

To the staff, writing community, and others I've met through the Institute of American Indian Arts: Derek Palacio, Claire Vaye Watkins, Pam Houston, Chip Livingston, Kim Blaeser, Ramona Ausubel, Marie-Helene Bertino, and many others.

A special thanks to Terese Mailhot, Casey Gray, and Tommy Orange for helping me through this process. No words are enough to express my gratitude.

To Clarion West and the Class of 2018 for the best summer of my life. May our stories be filled with stars and monsters and squids and smut.

To the Octavia E. Butler Society. Thank you for keeping her legacy alive and uplifting diverse voices.

To any teacher or professor whose had the misfortune to try to teach me. I've learned a lot, and I swear I'll turn in my homework one day.

To my professors at Bemidji State University who shaped my understanding of fiction, nonfiction, poetry, and life: Maureen Gibbon, Lauren Cobb, Larry Swain, Mark Christiansen, Jessica Durgan, and Carol Ann Russell.

All current and former staff at Bemidji State Upward Bound Program—Steve Berard, Kelly Steggall, Leah Girard—for believing in me and providing a path to success. My journey through college and to this book started from the steps of Birch Hall. Thank you.

No writing project of mine would be complete without the help of music. I'd like to thank the band Cloud Cult for making beauty out of pain and sharing it with the world.

To my best friend Autumn, who has stuck with me through laughter, tears, college, and late-night trips to Walmart. To Ethan, who more than anybody saw my writing evolution in real time. To Taylor, for always giving honest thoughts and advice on my work.

I'd like to express my love and gratitude to my family, who have always had endless patience for my whims and projects. This book was no different, and I couldn't be more grateful for everyone's support throughout the process.

To my sisters, Brittany and Samantha, who always know how to make me laugh.

To my brothers, Dimitri, Anthony, Miles, and Mackensie, who always inspire me to learn more about the world.

To my father, David, who has always worked hard to help everyone.

To my mother, Karen, who encouraged me to read everything I could.

Finally, to Sandy Mills. From the first page to the last, Jacob was never far from my mind while writing this book. Thank you for bringing such an amazing man into this world and keeping his memory alive for all those who loved him, near or far.

Miigwech

©John LaTourelle

DENNIS E. STAPLES is an Ojibwe writer from Bemidji, Minnesota. He graduated from the Institute of American Indian Arts with an MFA in fiction. He is a graduate of the 2018 Clarion West Writers Workshop and a recipient of the Octavia E. Butler Memorial Scholarship. His work has appeared in *Asimov's Science Fiction* and *Nightmare* magazine. He is a member of the Red Lake Nation. *This Town Sleeps* is his first book.